Thaumaturgic

By:

Merlin O'Toole

To George Lucas; who was the first writer to introduce me to the world of dystopia, and Suzanne Collins; who brought me back into it and showed me what it really is.

Contents

I- Kent Bernard

Change, most people would say, is a good thing. But others don't always accept this lightly. I learned this the hard way when I was caught that day, and my troubles were not over. Not by a long shot. My name is Kent Tavi Bernard, and I live in North Carolina, one of the thirteen states that made up the Thirteen Colonies. While the rest of the states are still the United States, the Thirteen Colonies are now the country of Nova Vega. I know what you're thinking: how can the United States still exist if the Thirteen Colonies formed Nova Vega? It's a really long story, but before I can explain it, I want to begin by telling you my story; a story filled with my share of troubles.

***

I was walking out of the First Citizens Bank with a wheelbarrow full of money bags. Yes, I'd been robbing banks for three years. I walked out through the front door. How did I do it without getting caught, you may ask? I'll get to that in a moment. It had been thirty-nine minutes since I had robbed the First Citizens Bank, and here I stood at the ruined bridge on what was once called Wayne Memorial Drive. This was the bridge that led back to my secret spot. What can I say? I couldn't deny the view. Several food restaurants and a movie theater to my left were in ruins. Some of them were decaying and crumbing, while the rest of the area was overgrown with plants. This was the one part of Goldsboro that non-security guards were not allowed to go to, but I went there anyway. It was peaceful, quiet, and calm, and it was the one place that allowed me some escape from all the rules enforced by the government itself. After my detour, I took another route, downhill to the right, to get to the other side of the ruined bridge uphill.

***

Wayne Community College had been out of business for over a century and was labeled condemned, but it made a great hiding spot when escaping law enforcement. The inside cafeteria merged from both the middle school and high school, and I used it as my camping site. I placed the money bags inside the ruined hot dog stand for safe keeping. Just when I was about to prepare some

1

dinner for myself, I noticed two teenage boys in ragged clothes standing at the glass doorway. One of them had dirty-brown hair with blue eyes, dark skin, and wore dirty, threadbare clothes with a big hole on the left side and just one shoe, on his left foot. The other boy had blonde hair, brown eyes, tan skin, and wore only shorts.

I looked over at my angel hair pasta, chicken, bottle of olive oil, and can of garlic, and then back at the boys. They looked as though they hadn't eaten in days and had nowhere to go. Despite being a runaway, I was not cruel. I couldn't refuse giving them hospitality.

"Would you boys like to join me for dinner?" I asked, smiling. "I'm making chicken pasta."

With smiles on their faces, they walked over to me as I started boiling the water before adding the angel hair pasta. I placed the boys in charge of watching the pot before cutting the chicken into cubic pieces and tossing them into the frying pan with some garlic. Once the pasta and the chicken were done, I mixed them together in one pan and finished with a drizzle of olive oil. Taking out three bowls and forks, I served each of us a generous portion. It tasted like ramen mixed with spaghetti, minus the meatballs and spaghetti sauce. Even the boys were enjoying it, eating quickly before licking the bowls to savor the taste. We ate until the pan was empty. We all wore delighted smiles on our faces. It had to be best meal we'd ever had.

"Now for dessert," I said while happily reaching for my backpack.

As I grabbed a bag of chocolate chip cookies, white chocolate pretzels, and brownies, I noticed, from the corner of my eye, the boys reaching for something in their clothes. I moved my shoulders up and back down. It was probably nothing. But when I turned around after taking the bag out, I stared in confusion upon seeing them holding guns and pointing them at me. I thought they were just toy guns at first, until I saw them smiling deviously. I rose my hands, my eyes widen with fear. A cold, nervous sweat broke out across my forehead. I froze in place, dropping the bag of goodies in the process.

"Okay, I get it. You're thieves. There's some money inside the hot dog stand. Just take it. It's yours."

Then, the boys changed. Not in personality, but in appearance. To my disbelief, they shape-shifted into police officers, taller and older. The thing that hadn't changed were those lethal guns pointed directly at me. They had the same hair, skin, and eye color as before, but now they both wore black police caps and light-purple uniforms with police badges on the right side of their chests. With my eyes still wide and my entire being engulfed in fear, I stared at them, wishing it was all a hallucination. I couldn't believe it. They had been Morphers, or Shape-Shifting Police Officers this whole time. I had just extended my hospitality to two police officers disguised as homeless children.

"Aww, crap," I said, as I closed my eyes and lowered my head in dismay.

***

Nova Vega was formed a year after the world was saved from the Global Cataclysm. How was it saved? Well, without warning, certain individuals developed mysterious powers. Nobody knows how it happened. Some say they were given powers by God. Others say that the mutations kicked in during the Global Cataclysm. Whatever their origin, a society with powers became common, while those without powers were rendered inferior. People with the same types of powers placed in different groups became known as Tribes, each of them unique and powerful.

There are the Resurrectors, or Returners; people with the power to revive the dead. They bring back those who are not ready to die. Hell, even God knows that most people don't deserve to die, especially those whose time has not yet come. So, people who possessed that power played the role of Savior for a time. After the Global Cataclysm, they were doctors during the days of Nova Vega. Well, one branch of doctors, technically. Unfortunately, a group of zealous fanatics protested against the idea of reviving the dead; whether old or young, believing it to be a disruption of the life and death cycle.

By the year 2070, the Resurrectors were condemned as heretics. Some managed to hide, nobody knew where, but the rest of them— men, women, and children— were hunted down, arrested, and executed via firing squad, hanging, and burning at the stake. Seven years later, through the demands of the fanatics, the Nova Vegan government condemned the power to revive the dead as heresy, declaring that only God, not man, could bring back the dead. Those who questioned the government and its laws ended up arrested and, if the law decided, executed. I know what you're going to say: you said "arrested and executed" twice! Well, that's because the Nova Vegan government is not like the government from the Days of Old. This government is cruel and manipulative, and it rules Nova Vega through fear.

Healers, the other branch of doctors, have the ability to cure various illnesses, diseases, and injuries. However, they can't cure disabilities. They tried on a person with High Functional Autism, and it didn't work. The person with High Functional Autism is me. My disability helped me mature faster with increased intelligence, but it also made me emotional, stubborn, and sometimes aggressive.

Another Tribe is the Shape-Shifters, most commonly known as Morphers. They can shape-shift into other people they know by memory and impersonate their voices. They're one of the branches of law enforcement, and often use that power to disguise themselves as criminals. While in school, Morphers are one of the branches in hall monitor duty, spying on delinquent students to see what rules they might be breaking. A majority of students don't like the idea. Not one bit. But one principal, handpicked by the Nova Vegan government, made it legal

3

for Morphers to be hall monitors, much to the students' dismay. And these are the same people that caught me back at the deserted community college.

Then, there are the Dimensional Travelers. They have the ability to create a portal leading to another world. You could say that they are a group of researchers gathering knowledge about different worlds' inhabitants, populations, histories, economies, and lifestyles. They used to bring back the information for educational purposes. However, like resurrection, dimensional travel was also condemned as heresy out of fear that the Dimensional Travelers would travel to the wrong place and bring back alien invaders. By 2039, thirteen of them escaped persecution, but the rest were massacred by the Morpher Police. In 2040, dimensional travel was declared heresy and forbidden. Tragic, I know. They killed the majority of the Dimensional Travelers; then forbade that power, even when none were left in Nova Vega.

Time Travelers also gathered information for educational purposes. Instead of traveling to another world, they travelled to another time period, finding out which modern historical theories were true and which were not true due to research flaws. Not everyone was able to accept the truth about history. Some stuck to the information they believed to be part of history. Upon seeing the disapproval of some of the citizens in Nova Vega, and out of fear that the Time Travelers would disrupt the timeline, in 2021, the government decided to lock them away for its country's protection. When they noticed how unsatisfied some of the citizens were, they decided to have them executed. Only four Time Travelers, two men and two women, escaped their execution by firing squad. They could've traveled through time, but they were locked within an execution room installed with an anti-Power field, preventing any prisoner from using their power. Time travel was the second power condemned as heresy in 2023.

Telepaths are a mind-reading group. They, as a special branch of law enforcement, specialize in reading apprehended criminals' minds to find out whether or not they have been telling the truth about their criminal acts. But the educational system had to put every classroom in an anti-Telepath field to prevent students with telepathy from copying off other students' works; despite knowing how to handle that power with responsibility. The anti-Telepath field was conceived in 2134 after one student was caught using telepathy in class. His name was Bart Parker, and he claimed that he couldn't control his power. The Nova Vegan Board of Education didn't believe him, even though they weren't Telepaths themselves. Whether he was telling the truth or not, and without any evidence to back him up, the Board had him expelled and created the anti-Telepath field. The development lasted for four years. It was completed five months before I was born. Unlike prison, the school allowed the use of powers, minus telepathy, so long as they didn't break the rules.

4

Nobody knew what happened to Parker after his expulsion, but the government led all of Nova Vega to believe that he hung himself out of guilt. The only evidence we saw was a suicide note. Even his parents didn't want to believe it. They were Telepaths themselves and claimed that the Nova Vegan government had lied. They interrogated late Nova Vegan President Caius Mussolitler in an attempt to uncover the truth. He refused to tell them anything and placed them under arrest for what he led the country to believe was the attempted assassination of the Nova Vegan President. Parents and grandparents were placed in prison until they submitted to the government's demands. Those who resisted were executed via hanging. Parker's parents were among those who resisted these demands and died protecting their son's honor. That made me hate the government even more. They chose fabrication over reality of the truth, making people, like Parker's parents, martyrs and heroes in the eyes of those who disagree with the government itself.

The Pyschokinesists, also known as Telekinesists, are the construction workers. A year after saving the world from the Global Cataclysm, they built the walls that now surround the Thirteen Colonial States. We were told the walls were built to keep those who had no powers out. Making us believe that the powerless were trying to invade Nova Vega, the Morphers shot them on sight. The Telekinesists created houses for only the middle and upper classes. Those of the lower class ended up exiled from Nova Vega for life. In 2022, during the Time Traveler Protest, the government had the Telekinesists build power-proof cells that prevented criminals of any possessed power from using powers, especially to escape.

I know I said that powers weren't allowed in prison, but I never said how. That's usually the tricky part when it comes to these explanations. And so, a year after the Telekinesists built power-proof cells, they made more equipment that prevented prisoners from using their power, like handcuffs, offices, and podiums.

The Seers are fortune-tellers. They determine the future for the Nova Vegan citizens. Those who had no future in Nova Vega were banished. People tried their best to prove the system wrong since they always believed that God was the only one who could predict the infallible future. There was a protest against the Seers in 2066, and after three years, most of them were cast out of Nova Vega. Some were shot on sight, while the rest fled in fear. Those who were revived by the sympathetic Returners after the shooting were killed a year later, leading to the Returner Manhunt. Not only were the Returners condemned as heretics, they were also labeled criminals for protecting those the government believed to have no purpose in life. They also condemned them as being a threat to the Seer Tribe. From that point on, the Seer Tribe was labeled legal in Nova Vega. I've got no opinions about them, but I do my best to avoid them and leave my future in my Maker's hands.

The Immortals are people who never age beyond sixteen to thirty years. They can do anything and everything career-wise. Rumor has it that they are God's selected people who were so loyal and faithful to Him that He granted them eternal life. They claimed that they'll remain alive until the end of the world. Sometimes, they even claim that after the end of the world, they'll keep their bodies when they return to Heaven. But in 2017, the Nova Vegan government viewed the Immortal Tribe as witches and warlocks, and condemned them as blasphemers and heretics, claiming that their immortality came from the Devil and that they were beacons to bring forth the Coming of the Antichrist. Some of them were injected with lethal poison, while the rest of the Tribe was banished. I always had mixed feelings about them. It makes me happy to not worry about death, but I also feel sad to think of their families and friends dying without them, unless they were Immortals, too.

Animators have the ability to create living things out of anything except corpses, since they're immune to their power. They are mostly entertainers, performing in educational shows, action movies, stand-up comedy, or soap operas. But some of the Animators are now considered back-up for law enforcement. In that department, the Animators can make super soldiers out of metal and iron. That's the cool part, in a non-threatening manner. Some even fear them for the use of their power. I would be afraid, too, if the Animators used their artificial army to intimidate me.

Element Manipulators can conjure up anything from any part of nature and a mixture of rocks and minerals, including toys, houses, and mostly weapons. Speaking of weapons, primarily they use their power to make guns, swords, and knives for law enforcement. Children who have that power can only make toy weapons. Preteens and teenagers can make both toy weapons and actual weapons. But when they reach twenty-one years of age, the Element Manipulators can no longer make toy weapons and always make the real deal. Not only can they conjure up weapons, but they can also dismantle them with their powers. They wouldn't want criminals to take the weapons from law enforcement. They can still make anything they desire, but weapons based on age change in time.

Flyers have the ability to fly to different parts of the world, but they are restricted to Nova Vega. Why, you ask? Well, anyone, including the Flyers, who attempt to breach the wall, end up shot dead on sight, whether by snipers, or missiles. The alarm system, installed during the construction of Nova Vega's surrounding wall, alerts anyone in law enforcement about any attempt to escape.

Anyway, to take flight, the Flyers sprout wings from their backs. They help with construction and law enforcement. As for students, they can use their power to fly to school whenever they don't want to be late. What better way to prevent getting a tardy?

Hypnotists, my Tribe, have the ability to hypnotize people with their eyes, making them do anything, such as coercing criminals into telling the truth. Hall monitors can do the same. There were criminals who used that power for selfish desires, and in 2064, the Nova Vegan government hired Telepaths to help law enforcement apprehend them, forcing them to wear blindfolds after handcuffing them. Hypnotists can even give criminals parole and are granted the power to put them back in prison should they commit crimes again. And that is how I was able to rob banks and shoplift stores without getting caught.

The last Tribe is the Teleporters. They can disappear from one place and reappear in another. Their careers vary depending on what they choose to do. Law enforcement is easy for them, especially when it comes to catching criminals. They can even help with construction by carrying heavy building materials to another part of the site.

"Óchidunámei" is what Nova Vegans call people who have no powers. When Nova Vega was created, these people were denied citizenship, and were left outside the walls to suffer and die. They looked to us for salvation, yet the government was cruel to them, forcing the country to believe that those without powers were dangerous, illegal aliens, and not welcome in Nova Vega. Whenever citizens of the United States with no powers seek help from Nova Vega, pleading because they are poor, or dying, or sick, the Nova Vegan government warns them to leave or die. They always refuse to leave and end up killed for defiance. It's horrible, and they don't deserve that kind of treatment. It was bad enough to restrict hospitality only to the upper- and middle-class citizens of Nova Vega, but denying the Óchidunámei was even worse.

***

"We've been looking for you for three years, Bernard. Your father is worried sick and has been the only one who hasn't given up on having you found," said the police officer with the dirty-brown hair. He placed me behind bars at the Goldsboro Police Department. "And this should teach you the dangers of shoplifting in stores and robbing banks."

"You will stay here for the night," said the police officer with the blonde hair. "Your father will be picking you up and dealing with you in the morning."

As the two police officers were about to leave, the one with the dirty-brown hair turned to me with a dry humorous, yet unpleasant smile and said, "And thanks for the chicken pasta. It was delicious."

I didn't respond. I felt angry and defensive, beating myself up over being duped by him and his partner. I supposed it could've been worse. I could've remained here for the rest of my life. Instead, they were keeping me in jail for just one night, much to my relief. Hated to imagine what my father's reaction would be when he found out I ran away from home and robbed a bank. It was not going to end well for me. Not by a long shot.

I climbed to the top bunk to get some rest, but not before I noticed graffiti in black marker on the ceiling. It said, "Down with the government! May the Maker protect us all!" It looked like someone hated the government and its cruel laws like I did. That made me smile, but only a little. Being thrown in jail does that. I drifted to sleep as my greenish-brown eyes slowly closed, and my body relaxed, becoming dead-to-the-world asleep.

***

That night, I had dreams. They were the same ones I always had. I was floating over a room that looked like a laboratory merged with a hospital operation room. People were there as well, but none of them saw me. I didn't know why. Some of them were in white lab coats, while others were wearing blue operation cloaks. Then, there were serums of different colors— white, green, orange, black, gray, red, yellow, blue, gold, pink, brown, sky blue, purple, silver, and rainbow. The people being injected screamed in pain, and there was a clock with the words at the bottom: Days, Hours, Minutes, and Seconds. One of the people in the lab coat said to the other, "We are running out of time!"

In the next part of the dream at the same place, there were some dead bodies— men, women, and children alike. The live ones were yelling and screaming, begging to be set free, but more people, possibly security guards due to the fact that they were wearing black uniforms, tased them into silence. Then, there was a woman lying on the operating table resembling a teenager, being young in appearance with long, brownish-red hair reaching her shoulders, a brown left eye, a blue right eye, a tattoo of a bald eagle on her right wrist, and two Greek Letters tattooed on her left wrist: A and Ω. She wore a light-green operation cloak. An old man dressed like a pastor with his face hidden in the shadow and wearing a silver crucifix around his neck stood above her at the head of the operating table, stroking her right cheek.

"Do not fear, my daughter," he said. "The Maker will protect you."

There was a rainbow serum within the injector and then there was loud banging.

***

I woke up startled and exhaustedly looked at the same officers who had thrown me in the slammer. The blonde-haired officer was banging impatiently on the bars with his baton.

"Wakey, wakey, eggs and bakey!" said the dirty-brown haired officer, who wore another cruel, yet humorous smile on his face.

"Aww, shit," I said, feeling exhausted as I got out of bed.

"Hey, watch your mouth, you money-stealing delinquent!" the blonde-haired officer scolded as he unlocked the jail cell while I walked over with my head down, hiding my shame and anger. "You're lucky you're going home. Be glad your father is bailing you out. Now, get your clothes, put them on, and get the hell out of our sight."

II- Kent Bernard

Once I had my clothes on, I finally saw my father again. It left me feeling dismayed. I lowered my head, a mixture of edginess and self-consciousness. My father's name was Jacob Aaron Bernard, and he was both the patriarch of the Hypnotist Tribe and a lawyer. I inherited his greenish-brown eyes. He wore a light-blue business suit with a purple tie and black dress shoes. However, I didn't inherit his light-brown hair color. I inherited my mother's red hair. I knew if I was ever caught, I'd be dealing with him first. He was both angry and disappointed at what I'd done.

In my defense, I'd only brainwashed the bank clerks into handing me six money bags. I didn't want to get too greedy, especially for my survival out in the streets. Even Nova Vega needed their share of the money. Had I stolen all of it, the society would have been reduced to poverty, and the system destroyed. It would've served the government right, but that would also make me no better than them. The irony was that even though I robbed them, I was also helping them at the same time. But after being arrested by Morpher Police Officers, my days as a runaway were over. And as punishment for my crime, I was denied breakfast for a day. When we left the police station, we got inside the black hover car that my father was driving. The talk was going to have to wait until we arrived back home, and I could tell by his angry expression that things were not going to end well.

***

At 400 Netherlands Valley Drive, the place that I ran away from three years earlier, there used to be other houses before the protests and the riots against the Nova Vegan government. Now, there were only three houses left in the neighborhood, with two others surrounding my house. The house itself had gray bricks and only one floor level. The roof was black with a dark-red chimney at back, smack dab in the middle, and the garden had only red roses in front of the window outside the living room.

As we got inside the house, my father forced me to sit on the dark-purple couch in the living room, only adding to my discomfort and fear. Instead of looking at him, I stared at the dark wooden coffee table in front of me. I felt like I was back at the police station, and the living room was the interrogation room. I may not have been in one before since I only spent one night in jail, but I had seen some on crime shows long before I ran away. The big difference being our living room was now the interrogation room and had only a bad cop and no good cop.

After a long time of silence, my father shouted at me that he was sick and tired of "all of this stubbornness," as he said, that I pulled three years back. His shouting startled me, making me jump a little. It was the first time I'd felt this afraid. How could he remember that I was still missing after three years? Normally, parents would've forgotten about their missing children after a long amount of time. But my family was known to have photographic memories, and my father was more fixated on finding me than focusing on his job. Should I have been glad, or skeptical?

"Your frequent crimes nearly cost me my job as a lawyer, Kent Tavi Bernard!" he shouted.

Nope, definitely not glad. He was fixated on looking for me just to save his reputation and his career. Man, what a selfish bastard!

"Sometimes, you have to bend the rules a little," I responded morosely. "Besides, a teenager has got to eat when living on the streets, and what I did, I did to survive. Is that a problem?"

"Actually, yes," Dad said banging his fist on the coffee table. "Stealing is against the law, and on top of that, you ran away from home! You didn't just break one law, but two! What gave you the right to run away?"

Try getting into a second marriage too soon, I would've answered. I refused to answer him, knowing how he would react if I did.

"Answer me when I ask you a question," he yelled.

What was the point? I was already in trouble for running away, not to mention all the thievery. Again, if I answered, I would end up facing his wrath more. Yet silence didn't seem to be the answer, either. The longer I remained silent, the angrier my father became. His face grew red, hinting at one huge explosion. Rather than hitting me, he picked up the coffee table like an enraged gorilla and threw it at the wall to my right. The table smashed into the family photos hanging between the two tall windows, shattering the glass from the picture frames. The only photo that fell to the floor was of my mother, who died a year before I ran away. My heart stopped in shock, and I felt tears spring to my eyes upon seeing it crash to the floor. When I stared at my mother's image, my throat closed up. She'd once had beautiful red hair, bluish-green eyes, fair skin, and lips as red as rose petals. She wore the same warm smile that I would never see again, and had the same hair color as mine, which I would always keep to remind me that my mother would always be with me.

My father looked back at me just in time to notice my sad expression. He walked up to me and leaned his face toward mine. The look in his eyes showed nothing but anger and disappointment. I was afraid of him, and he told me that I should be as he straightened.

"Go to your room, Kent," he growled. "No meals for you for the rest of the day, and you're grounded for a month."

Things were never the same without Mom. If she'd been alive, she would never have allowed this to happen. She would've held me close and told me that everything would be alright. Dad would retain his calm demeanor thanks to her, since she knew how to keep his happiness alive. But with her gone, those days were over, and his reason to stay happy was no more.

I marched back to the coat room, where my father and I had come in through earlier, went to the hallway, and turned left to my bedroom. It has been three years since I'd been in my own bedroom. There was a large window at the back wall sandwiched between my bed on the right and my computer desk on the left. To the left of the bed was a bookcase attached to it, while the clothes cabinet was at the right. Above the bed was the old clubhouse my father made when I was seven, back when he was a nice person, like my mother. It was the only place where I could play with my toys and read books. Next to the door was a widescreen television connected to the wall with a DVD player on top of the miniature gray entertainment center that was half my height. Inside the entertainment center was my alphabetized DVD collection. The room contained a white dining table with a long lamp in front of the trashcan and a recycling bin at the left of the computer desk. On the computer desk was my white laptop with a USB connector for the wireless mouse, and a black laptop cooler under the laptop with my printer on the left and my smartphone on the right.

It felt good to be back in my cozy bedroom, but I already missed being at the abandoned community college, which was depressing to me. It was much better there than being under my father's roof. I wanted to go back, but I would end up getting caught again, and next time, my father wouldn't bail me out.

***

Later that mid-morning, while lying face-down on my bed, staring at the wall, my stomach began growling since I hadn't eaten any breakfast. I sat up straight with my arms around my bent legs, balling up like a baby in his crib. I wasn't sure what else to do. Not a day went by where I didn't miss having Mom around, and my world was already falling apart. So, I took a book from the bookcase that my mother gave me on my twelfth birthday five years back— The Hunger Games.

I'd always felt sorry for the people who had to live under the rule of their autocratic government, eating scraps and participating in the death game. Too bad they didn't have powers, otherwise, they would've done the same thing I'd done when I ran away from home. They wouldn't have had to go hungry again.

By the time my mother died, a year after giving me the books, I had read the whole book trilogy four times. Now, just when I was getting to the part where the male character gave the bread to the female character, I heard the door opening. I looked, and it was Gabriella, my sister. The last time I saw her, she was an eleven-year-old girl with pigtails. Now, she could be our mother's twin sister, but she was fourteen and parted her hair to the right instead of in the middle, and she wore no lipstick. Seeing her again made me warm and happy. She was holding something inside a large napkin.

"Hey, Kent," she said with a smile on her face. "It's been a while."

"Yes, it has," I responded, closing the book and placing it on my bed.

Gabriella removed the napkin, revealing a plastic plate of scrambled eggs, toast and jam, and hash browns. She took something out from her dress, which turned out to be a box of chocolate milk with a bendy straw. The plastic fork and knife were already set up, and my sister, already aware of our father's behavior, told me to eat quickly before he came out of his room. I did as I sat at my dining table, grateful to be enjoying a breakfast I hadn't eaten in three years. It seemed she had our mother's touch, since Mom used to make breakfast just the same way.

And when I finished, I gave her the empty plate with the used napkin, fork, knife, and empty chocolate milk box, thanking her for the meal. She told me before she left that she would come back into my room with lunch later. I believed her, and when she left the room, I went back to my bed and continued with the book.

***

Four hours later, Gabriella snuck in a peanut butter and jelly sandwich with lactose-free milk. I was amazed to see that she remembered to toast the bread first. She knew I loved butter toasted bread before making a sandwich. Like mother, like daughter, as I would say. I would definitely count on her if I needed her.

***

Six hours later, she brought in a plastic plate of salmon with Brussel sprouts, squash, zucchini, and a plastic cup of milk. It was good to know that she brought in food for me without getting caught by our father, hence being a lookout for him, if she ever saw him on the way to my room. I asked her how he was not able to notice the smell despite my punishment. She told me that she "hypnotized him into thinking that one-month grounding was punishment enough." That was a relief. While I was eating, Gabriella asked, "Why did you run away from home, and what's this about stealing to survive when you could've gotten a job to earn a living?"

"The Nova Vegan government can only allow college graduates to get jobs," I answered. "They didn't give me a choice. I didn't want to risk banishment from

13

Nova Vega. I could've been banished for stealing, but with Dad being the patriarch of our Tribe, he wouldn't allow it; wanting to deal with me himself. And I ran away because I didn't like the idea of Dad marrying another woman after Mom died. It was too soon for me," I said, tears starting to drip from my eyes. "I wasn't ready to have a stepmother! If Mom were alive, she would be ashamed of me for what I did! Can you blame me for not accepting a stepmother a year after our mother's death? But then again, I'm angry at the government more! If they hadn't condemned the Returners, Mom would still be alive, and I wouldn't have run away from home!"

I put my head down in both shame and sadness, and Gabriella, out of pity, held me from behind to comfort me. For three years, she hadn't understood how I could run away from home, stealing to survive.

Don't be sad, my little star,
I am always here for you,
Whether we are near or far,
I know that you will come through.

The world is the darkest night,
And its shadows will dwell on,
But I'm your eternal light
That will bring you to your dawn.

Do not fear, my little star,
You must look to the far north,
While you hold your starry spar,
This path will now bring you forth.

I am the light that shields you
From the darkest shadow's mind,
There is no need to feel blue,
Our lights will be intertwined.

Everything will be alright,
The brightest star will call you forth,
And he will be here tonight,
He'll come by from there up north.

Our hopes will never be gone
As long as we are aligned,
Our trails are the path of dawn,
This path is not far behind.

Don't be sad, my little star,
I am always here for you,
Whether we are near or far,
I know that you will come through.

That song, "Little Star's Dawn," was the same one our mother used to sing to me before I went to sleep, bringing me comfort when I was sad or scared. It cheered me up a little, but it still wasn't the same without her.

"If it's any consolation," Gabriella said, "Hestia is a nice woman, and she would never replace our mother. Not now, not ever."

"It doesn't matter," I responded bitterly. "There's still no taking back what I've done and why I did it."

"That's true. But if you explain to Dad what you told me, I'm sure he'll understand."

"Oh, trust me. He doesn't go back on his punishments. Knowing him, once the punishment is set, there will be no changing it, let alone revoking it. Not even hypnosis can work the second time. He might notice."

"Kent, you'll never know until you try. Just be glad that you are going to the twelfth grade."

"Yeah, even runaways need an education." I finished my dinner and milk. "Normally, they wouldn't want anything to do with school. They don't call it homeschool for nothing. I should be glad the government didn't outlaw *that*, too."

"The choice of education depends on the person who ran away from home," she took the empty plate and plastic cup. "Don't worry about what Dad says. Just give him a good chat, and if he doesn't change the punishment, at least you will have managed to explain to him what happened. Now, go get washed up. We have a big day tomorrow."

That big day made me nervous at first since I was a juvenile delinquent as a runaway. I just hoped that school wouldn't treat me badly after what I had done the past three years. They would probably have me repeat ninth grade, even though I had already taught myself all the way to the eleventh grade.

As my sister left the room, I took off my t-shirt, black shoes, and jeans and put on my blue pajamas. On my way to the bathroom across the hall, something jumped on me, and I fell over in surprise. It was my dog, Primrose; Siberian Husky/German Shepherd mix. She had the Siberian husky hair color with blonde on top of her head like a Mohawk and dark-blue eyes. I was happy to see her again as I ruffled the back of her head. My sister gave her to me on my twelfth birthday and I named her after one of the characters from the book trilogy I got on the very same day. I nicknamed her Rosy because I thought it was cute. Last time I saw her, she was a puppy, but now she was already five years old. It was good to be reunited after three years, and I leaned my face into her black and white fur, feeling how soft it was. With my arms around Rosy, and Gabriella's words still ringing in my ears, it didn't seem so bad to be home again.

III- Phoebe Truman

Kent's life out on the streets was filled with insecurities, but my life was even more complicated, full of struggles and torment. All my life, I'd known nothing but pain and suffering, with only my family supporting me and helping me out through thick and thin. 143 years after the Global Cataclysm, and more families had more expectations than support for their children. It made me sad to see most families being unsupportive while children were expected to fend for themselves, though not all of them had the capability to do so, thanks to the government and its cruel laws.

Before I met Kent, I was a victim of bullying, and a loner. I was incapable of standing up for myself, had trouble making friends, and I was unsociable around people, with the exception of my older brother Ferenc and our parents. My name is Phoebe Bridget Truman, and my story begins with the first day of school, before my classes started and before I met Kent.

***

I am from the Flyer Tribe, and my parents are the patriarch and matriarch of that Tribe. One day, they left my brother in charge of me while they went away on a business trip, but they were gone for about a year. Ferenc told me I should not worry about what their fates held or assume the worst. Before I went to school, I flew to the top of Goldsboro Water Tower and sat down, retracting my wings.

My wings were as white as a dove. I wore my hair in a long, dark-brown ponytail. I have hazel eyes and usually wear a light-purple school uniform gown with long, white socks reaching six inches above my black shoes. Whenever I go to the top of the water tower, I imagine myself soaring in the clouds and feeling the warm wind blowing on my smiling face. And yes, the school we went to required school uniforms. Not just private schools but also public schools. The school I go to, Rosewood High, was not the school like in the Days of Old. After the Global Cataclysm, strict laws were enforced, leading to a political controversy, including the requirement of school uniforms. The uniforms were based on gender, like the uniform I'm wearing, which was for girls. It made me

17

upset that I wasn't allowed to wear whatever I wanted to school. If they hadn't done that, things would've been different. That would make me feel better and happy.

As for the boys, they wear light-blue business clothes with black ties and black shoes. And that was what my older brother Ferenc was wearing when he snuck up on me out of nowhere. He had brown hair, blue eyes, and smiled like a child whenever he scared the hell out of me. His wings were black, like a jackdaw's. There went my morning view of Goldsboro, the right half still stabilized from the gallows to the bank, while the left half was in ruins from the bridge to the community college.

"Hey, Fly Girl!" he said, startling me so my eyes widened in surprise.

It was, in fact, the first thing I heard from behind. I jumped in fright and extended my wings before I fell off the water tower. He laughed in amusement, much to my irritation, while I hovered in midair.

"Damn it, Ferenc!" I yelled. "You're lucky we can fly, or I would have ended up splattered on the ground."

"Oh, come on, Sis, lighten up. I was just messing around."

"And messed up my morning routine."

"Oh?"

"Yeah."

I landed back on the top, retracted my wings, and looked back at the town. It was one of the few places that hadn't fallen into ruins like the rest of Wayne County. Ferenc, much to my reluctance, decided to sit with me after retracting his wings. I usually didn't mind being alone, and I didn't like the idea of Ferenc being at my side. Being alone with no one but him was usually a pain, but for once, I had to make an exception. He had his moments of being protective of me. If anything were to happen to me, he would defend me, even though I took pride in trying to fight my own battles, much to his doubt. My brother might be a pain, but he's alright.

There was no denying the view from on top of the water tower. The sun always looked radiant in the morning, shining on windows as they reflected gleaming light. Unless there was rain, with or without thunderstorms, the morning itself was nice, warm, and beautiful. And after spending over an hour watching the sun rise over the horizon, it was time for me to get to school.

I stood up and extended my wings from my back. Before I could fly anywhere, Ferenc grabbed my left arm. I looked at him curiously, "What? I have to get to school. First day of class starts in thirty minutes."

"I know," he said, as he stood up and extended his wings with a smile on his face. "But wanna race there, like old times?"

It was a tradition that my brother set up when he was eight years old, and I was four going on five. Every first day of school, we would race to see who could get there first. The loser would have to do the winner's homework for a week. Ferenc won the first two times, but I won against him once. It's like most people say, *"Third time's the charm."* But when he was eleven, and I was seven going on eight, we got into trouble by our parents. They were worried that if we did each other's homework, we wouldn't be learning anything. We never did the Ferenc Truman Flight Race again.

And after six years, my brother wanted to bring it back. The only problem being he was a college student, and if he won, I would have to do his difficult assignments. But I'm a fast learner, and I'd been doing work above my school level since I was a toddler. This would be easy as pie. Besides, how could I refuse a challenge? I smiled confidently and responded, "You're on! Get ready to lose, Fly Boy!"

"Let's see what you got, Fly Girl!"

We ascended from the water tower and flew to the east, attempting to see whose flight was better.

***

Rosewood High School was the same as before the Cataclysm; the same brick building almost like a college, excluding the dormitories and long walks from class to class, same parking lot at two sides and the front, same sports fields at two sides and behind, and same locker room building between the baseball field and the football field. Instead of the United States of America flag on the flagpole, the school used a new flag that had been around for over a century. The Nova Vega Flag was red on the left and purple on the right, and the emblem in the middle was a silver shield inside the golden sun with two swords crossed together- one black from top left to bottom right; tip of the blade to the hilt, and the other white behind the black sword, but the tip of the blade top right and the hilt bottom left.

According to the Nova Vegan government, the country itself was the only livable place left on the planet. No one knew how it had happened. Outside the walls was a vast wasteland, where the exiled and the Óchidunámei were sentenced to suffer and die. It was one country before the Global Cataclysm. But just about all of the United States was reduced to nothing but complete ruins, and even after eighty-five years, it hadn't changed. There was no life, no vegetation, no animals—nothing but destroyed buildings, dying plants and trees, and depleted oceans. There was no telling what had happened to the rest of the planet, but we were led to believe that it had died along with the United States, whether it was the war after the Cataclysm, or the plague, or even environmental disasters. Either way, Nova Vega became the only inhabitable place left.

Anyway, my brother and I landed on the school grounds at the same time, resulting in a tie for the first time. When the race ended with both winners, Ferenc and I decided that we didn't have to do each other's homework.

"Don't forget, Sis," he said with a confident smile. "I'll get you next year."

"If Mom and Dad are not home by then, I'll be waiting," I said, smiling.

"Agreed. See you after school."

"Likewise."

Before he had a chance to depart to North Carolina State University, we were taken by surprise by a cruel, unfriendly face. Sirena Galiena Peyton. Her hair was as brown as dirt, eyes as green as grass, lips as red as blood, and she was in her Teleporting Hall Monitor uniform. The uniform was like a police officer's uniform from the Days of Old, only black. With her pen and notepad at hand, she looked at me with an angry, cruel smile on her face and said, "Hey, Truman! You know the rules: no standing on the grass! That's a demerit!"

"Sirena, school has not started yet," I said in irritation. "Hall monitors are not supposed to do that until then."

"Well, that's too damn bad! As an aspiring law enforcer, it is my duty to punish criminals and rule breakers, whether school has started or not! And speaking of rule breaking," she looked at my brother, "isn't he too old for high school?!"

"We were only racing to school," Ferenc answered in annoyance with his arms crossed over his chest. "There's nothing wrong with having a friendly game."

"Oh, you like games, huh?" Sirena placed her pen in her notepad before putting them away in her pocket. "Well, come to think of it, that sounds like fun."

She gave us a false smile, walking up to him and placing her left arm around his shoulders, asking innocently, "Where do you go to school?"

"NC State University. Why?"

"Well, since Phoebe and I have ten minutes to spare, I got a brand-new game we can play."

"Really?" he asked in a suspicious tone.

"Yep. It's called…"

She and my brother teleported right before my eyes. I felt terrified. This was not happening. It was bad enough she had to bully me around, but teleporting Ferenc against his will? Not wanting to wait around for her to return, I rushed over to the entrance, only to come across her appearing before me, blocking my path. She wagged her index finger and said, "Ah, ah, ah! No running on school grounds, Truman!"

She took out her notepad and pen and wrote another minus sign under my name. That was so not fair! Another demerit before school even started?! How mean and authoritative could one hall monitor be? No, she was a bully who pushed her authority too far. At least things couldn't get any worse, I thought. With my eyes widened in fear, I asked, "What did you do to my brother?"

"Oh, just a little game of swirly," she answered in an innocent tone. "And as for you…"

With a cruel smile on her face, she grabbed me by the collar and teleported us to who knew where. Things were about to get ugly.

IV- Phoebe Truman

This was both brutal and humiliating. Sirena teleported the two of us into the janitor's closet, which happened to be locked. It was small with a boiler at the left opposite from the door, and the cleaning supplies with mops and brooms were at the right. It smelled like toilet water and gym socks, much to my disgust. She pulled my bangs before proceeding to give me the baton at the back of my left leg and slapping me across the face, causing me to scream in extreme pain. Then, she tied me up to a chair and taped my mouth to silence the scream. She gave me one last wicked smile and said, "A tardy will be punishment enough for you. But don't worry. I'll be back after first period, so you will come out when you've learned your place."

She vanished before my eyes, and it was only five minutes before homeroom. And with my leg broken, there was no way of moving to the door to get attention. I was helpless, and I was going to miss the beginning of the first day, and history class. Like I said, it was brutal and humiliating.

But another Teleporter appeared. He was fit in tone and had short, dark-brown hair and blue eyes. His name was Seifer Valentine, and unlike Sirena, he was one of the nice Teleporters and my friend. He must've heard me screaming. That's how he appeared out of nowhere. He untied me, removed the tape from my mouth, and, to my relief, teleported the both of us to homeroom.

***

Five minutes before school started, we were in the art classroom. There were six large desks that formed a square all around, and four chairs for each desk. My friends Seifer, Mark Delsin, and Valeda Lombardi and I were at the desk near the indoor window next to the door leading in and out of the classroom. Mark was an Animator, slightly chubby with muscle girth, dark skin, black braided hair, and brown eyes. Valeda was a Healer, hence her hand glowing green upon using her powers to heal my leg. She had tan skin, red hair, and hazel eyes. Apart from Seifer, Mark and Valeda had been with me since I'd moved to Goldsboro the day after my eleventh birthday. Since then, we had been inseparable, even causing trouble, mostly to piss off the Nova Vegan government, such as laxative

22

pranks in coffee to Morpher Police Officers, dropping paint balloons on political officials, and exploding pen bombs to splatter ink on Chancellor Jelen's face. We were children. It was in our nature to cause mischief, like most children do.

I used to a loner and constantly bullied as a child, yet I now have friends by my side. I know loners don't usually have friends, but this is different. Seifer, Mark, and Valeda were the only friends I'd ever made, and one other friend, which I will get to in the moment. Causing mischief was my way of venting my frustration and anger, since I was incapable of standing up to my bullies. Every time I tried to stand up to bullies like Sirena, even trying to avoid a conflict, I always ended up getting beaten into submission. Being around my friends made me feel like an extrovert, and whenever I got into a conflict that I tried to stay out of, they would comfort me like Ferenc did. The difference being they backed out of a fight with my bullies, while my brother did not.

"Phoebe, you really need to start standing up for yourself," said Valeda with her Mexican Accent. "I won't always be there to heal your injuries every time Sirena inflicts pain on you."

"Leda is right," said Mark, who had a Jamaican Accent. "And you can't vent your anger on the government forever. It's only going to get harder for you."

"It's not my fault the Nova Vegan Board of Education picked Sirena as the hall monitor, and they don't do a damn thing about bullies here at school, thanks to their incompetence," I said. "And FYI, I tried to stand up for myself a couple of times before, when I chose not to stay out of a conflict, but it always backfired."

"True, but we won't always be there to help you out," said Seifer. "Besides, if you think Sirena is bad, just watch out for the Emmerich Brothers. They're the worst."

My eyes widened in fear. "The Emmerich Brothers?"

"The Nova Vegan Disciplinary Duo selected by the Board to help Sirena out."

Seifer explained that the Emmerich Brothers had moved from the former Washington D.C.-turned-Imperia to Goldsboro just last summer. They were trained at Imperia Cadet Military Academy and were top of the class. The brothers were arrogant, ruthless, and dangerous. The worst part about them: they were Morphers, and they used any method of punishment, even getting away with murder, or execution in their case. And since they were transferring to Rosewood High School by order of the Nova Vegan government, all hell was about to break loose in our lives. I wouldn't want to encounter them. Sirena as my only bully was bad enough for me. The Emmerich Brothers would be even worse.

"And they're very unpredictable," said Seifer, looking directly at me. "So, be wary when you encounter them. They can appear as anyone, even as your friends and family."

"Why not just test them to find out about it, or talk about something they don't know?" I asked.

"Because when they were in the academy, they were trained to avoid that kind of trick. But do it too long, they are likely to snap, which can blow their cover."

"And if there wasn't an anti-Telepath field installed in every school throughout Nova Vega, it would've been too easy, Mon," said Mark.

Before we had a chance to continue our conversation, the bell rang, and everyone, including the four of us, stopped talking. Our homeroom teacher, Lisa Strickland, was also the art teacher- dark skin, dark-red hair reaching her neck, brown eyes, and she wore a purple business suit with a skirt, gold tie, glasses, and black high-heel shoes. She was compassionate and kind to her students, which always made me smile. For the first ten minutes, she discussed the rules of the school, the Nova Vegan Pledge, and the National Anthem. You don't want to know about the second and third parts. But all I can say is it had nothing to do with freedom or living together as equals, and it was all about unlimited order, infinite loyalty to the government, and nothing about God being above us all, leaving me pissed off.

***

Seifer and I had our first period class together from our teacher Bill Bayne- short, black hair, brown eyes, and, like me and Seifer, fair skin, and he wore a gray business suit with a black tie and black shoes. According to him, our universe was originally known as Libra before the Global Cataclysm. A month after that event, Libra became Perditus, a ruined world. Nova Vega was all about order, while the rest of the planet fell into chaos. The name Libra was given to remind us of what the world was like before Nova Vega existed with most of us granted powers.

Sitting behind me and Seifer was another friend of mine— Asteria Kelly, a member from the Morpher Tribe- long, black hair reaching down shoulder-length, hazel eyes, fair skin, and she has rosy cheeks and some dimples.

During the 2nd of February in the year 1 A.R., the first year after the rise of Libra/Perditus, otherwise known as 2013 A.D., Nova Vega was officially founded. The walls were built to keep the remnants of the world out. But it was also the day she, Seifer, Mark, Valeda, and I would gaze at the stars from the top of Goldsboro Water Tower.

She told us that once every twenty-nine years, a rare Aurora Borealis would appear all around the planet for both the Northern and Southern Hemisphere to see. It appeared in a rainbow color, which, according to legend, would give new life, new love, and new hope to replace the ones that were lost. The last Aurora Borealis occurred in 2128, also known as 116 A.R., and the next one was only two years away, but would last for seven days. No worries about that. There was always time to see two or three more of those occurrences in our lifetime.

***

After school, the five of us decided to go to Hestia's Diner to eat. It was the only food place we could think of, and it was where the old diner, Boyette's Eagles Nest Diner, used to be; next door to the two-floor apartment. It was right across the street from Rosewood Middle School. It was founded three years after Nova Vega was founded, and damn, they had the best veggie burgers in town. Seifer was into hot dogs in manna-made buns. Mark liked fruit salad. Valeda would have mac and cheese with salad. Asteria's favorite was grilled chicken with corn and lettuce.

***

Three years earlier- We usually sat at the counter in front of the six dining booths, across from the grill, with the kitchen door next to it, fryer, and oven. There was also a television set. A human-sized black radio broadcasted the Nova Vegan International News, while behind it were the restrooms. The floor was checkered in black and white, the ceiling was gray, and the wall's bottom was green with the top yellow.

The waitress that served us was Hestia Bernard, the owner of the diner- long, black hair reaching her shoulders, violet eyes, tan skin, a beauty mark under her right eye, and she wore a purple short-sleeve shirt with a gold skirt, a white apron, a blue headband, and black high-heel shoes. Her name and the name of the diner was just a coincidence. Back then, she was known as Hestia Rohan until she got married two weeks after getting engaged. Hestia was a very suitable owner for the place. But her small smile indicated some trouble.

"What's wrong?" Seifer asked in concern.

"Oh, it's nothing, really," Hestia said.

"Ms. Rohan, we can tell something is wrong," Mark said sternly.

"Yeah, you can tell us," said Asteria. "We won't say a word."

She was a bit reluctant at first, but eventually she told us about what happened the day after her engagement six days earlier. The boy that would become her stepson had run away from home, and the police were searching for him but found no sign of him. We were told that he was probably upset over his father speed dating and getting into marriage a year after his wife passed on. Hestia was not into fast engagements, but didn't have any other choice. In truth, she didn't really blame the boy for running away from home. A father getting into another relationship after his wife's funeral and then getting married a year later was too soon. Even she agreed that the government's laws were cruel and unfair, and that the only way for her soon-to-be stepson to make a living was through stealing, and hopefully he would educate himself if he was to survive in the streets.

I did feel pity for the boy. Wherever he ran away to, I hoped that he was having a good life. Perhaps it would be better if the police didn't find him. Better for him to be left alone than living with a father who rushed into things too quickly, and who could blame him? If my father had done that after my mother passed on, I'd have done the same thing.

***

Present- Before we had a chance to get there for the usual order, our path was blocked by Sirena in front of the fire station. To our gaping shock, she was not in the best of moods. She must've noticed that I hadn't stayed in the janitor's closet for all of first period. Why else would she already be in a bad mood? To my horror, she had three additional members with her. She called it her Teleporter Gang.

"Alright, Truman!" she yelled, pointing at me in fury. "I told you that I would let you out of the janitor's closet after first period, and you weren't there! If I can't punish you the easy way, then I'll punish you the hard way!"

She snapped her fingers, and three of her minions proceeded forward, ready to beat me to a bloody pulp. There was no point in flying away from the problem since they would only capture me quickly before I would have a chance. So, Seifer, Mark, Valeda, and Asteria stood in the way in their attempt to protect me.

"Get the hell out of the way!"

"Make us, bitch!" Mark snarled, as he cracked his knuckles before making a battle stance.

"You want Phoebe, you'll have to get past the four of us!" said Asteria in her Canadian Accent.

"Thanks for the tip, Two-Face," said Sirena, who smiled a wicked grin. "Send them away, my minions! I'll warm this weakling up until you return!"

They did what she said and teleported my friends somewhere. What frightened me was that I had no way of knowing where they were. It was the same stunt she'd pulled on Ferenc, except it was somewhere at NC State University for him. I wasn't sure where they were teleported to. Sirena took out her extended baton and beat me on the back, causing me to fall over on the ground. I screamed in pain again, and again. I was too afraid to fly away. No matter how many times I wanted to back away, or stand up for myself, there was no point. Her Teleporter Gang returned and proceeded with more beating after my bully did her part. Tears leaked from my eyes, the pain overwhelming me. Then, I heard a voice, "Hey!"

They looked in the direction the voice was coming from. "Leave her alone! She's already suffered enough!"

V- Kent Bernard

The first day of school wasn't so bad, except having to take a trip to the principal's office as he looked through my criminal records. The principal of Rosewood High School was Oswald White, the patriarch of the Morpher Tribe- dark skin, amber eyes, had a completely shaven head. He wore a purple business suit with a silver tie and black business shoes. He told me when I first met him that he, himself, was the brother of one of the police officers that had arrested me two days before. Unlike his brother, the principal had a no-nonsense personality, but used it more so than the former. Principal White's expression was like an angry bull.

"Consider yourself lucky your father is a lawyer," he said in a strict, but calm tone. "And be glad that despite being a juvenile delinquent, you homeschooled yourself for the past three years. So, I'm going to cut you a break, but consider this your first and last warning. If I ever find out you're committing another crime, especially on school grounds, I will not hesitate to have you expelled and arrested. And next time, your father will not set you free," he leaned toward my tense face. "Do I make myself clear?"

"Perfectly," I said.

"Good," he leaned back, took out a school uniform, and gave it to me. "Put *these* on in the restroom and get to homeroom. You have ten minutes."

My homeroom was in chemistry class, and first period was English. When I was twelve, back when I'd first read *The Hunger Games*, I wanted to be a fiction writer myself. But after running away from home, all I'd ever known was cruelty, mistreatment, and discrimination. That's what happened when the government forbade students who were not college graduates from getting jobs; both full-time and part-time. So, I wasn't given a choice but to live a life of crime in order to survive.

The books from the Days of Old were kept, but by the time 2025 occurred, fiction writing was no longer possible and became forbidden in Nova Vega, which was decreed by the government itself on the very same year. The people in it feared that fiction writing would start a revolution and bring equality back to the country. Keeping the old books was fine to them, as long as new books weren't

27

written. Unfortunately, the books that were kept had censored out anything involving rebellion against corrupt governments and their leaders. It buried any hope that they deemed a threat. If my mother hadn't snuck *The Hunger Games* to me on my birthday, I would never have known the dark side of life, reality, and the world around us, nor would I be inspired to learn more about our government's mistreatment of society. Regardless of being inspired, my dream of being a fiction writer was crushed upon learning about its dissolution during English.

I wasn't sure what to do for a career. Would I become a lawyer, a police officer, a detective, a counselor, a doctor, or a therapist? I didn't know what decision to make. Being a member of the Hypnotist Tribe, my choices were limited, as it was with the other Tribes. But to me, none of them would ever appeal to my future. If I refused, or chose a different career outside of what was based on my Tribe, I would be banished. For now, I would have to stay focused on my schoolwork. I was also glad that no one else in the school knew about my life in the streets, or they would hate me before I even got a chance to let them know my side of the story. Then again, some of them might agree with me. I didn't know. I would never know unless I got to know them first.

***

After school, Gabriella and I were about to head straight home. I was still grounded after all. But my sister did have a point when she said that I should give our father a good chat. It would be nice to share my insecurities with him, get it off my chest. What if he didn't believe me? What if, even though I reasoned with him, I was proven right and Gabriella wrong? I was sweating, drowning in a mixture of fear and insecurity. I didn't want to know what the outcome would be. *Stop torturing yourself, Kent. Like your sister said, "You'll never know until you try." Just have a chat with him, and everything will be alright.*

Before we could walk further, I heard voices coming from behind us, "Alright, Truman!"

There were five teenagers being confronted by none other than Sirena. She had three new minions to back her up. Two years before I ran away from home, she was crushing on me. She'd always misunderstood the concept of love, and like she did with rules, she had a tendency to push things too far. I tried my very best to ignore her secret love notes, avoid her at lunch time, and free time at the library, but she crossed the line by blurting out her "declaration of love" for me in front of the entire school. Everyone laughed at both of us, students and teachers alike. She didn't care, but I did. And I was so angry that I used my hypnosis to make everyone forget what they'd heard. Before she had a chance to blurt it out again, I dragged her outside the building and underneath the stairs, told her she was "making a scene and going too far."

I was going to hypnotize her to stop her unhealthy obsessive love, but she teleported to avoid my power. We got caught by the middle school principal and ended up banned from the end-of-the-year school dance for "harassment and abusing one's powers." That was the bad news. The good news was that it kept me from seeing Sirena there, who was angry and bitter at me for what I'd done. I didn't have a choice, because she didn't give me one. She was pushy, self-obsessed, and controlling. There is an old saying that sometimes, no good deed goes unpunished. And it was worth it. I never saw her again after that, until now.

"I told you that I would let you out of the janitor's closet after first period, and you weren't there!" she yelled. "If I can't punish you the easy way, then I'll have to punish you the hard way!"

Gabriella and I witnessed her snapping her fingers, signaling her minions to go after the girl I'd never met before. But I did know the other two; Seifer Valentine and Mark Delsin. I haven't seen them in four years, not since my mother's funeral. The other two girls I didn't recognize. However, I did notice the four of them defending the girl that Sirena called Truman.

Just as Seifer, Mark, and the other two girls tried to protect Phoebe, Sirena's minions had teleported them away against their will while she proceeded to beat her in the back multiple times with her own baton. I was so angry at the sight of what that girl was doing that I moved to tell her off. Gabriella grabbed me by the right arm and said, "Kent, don't. It's not worth it."

"Sis, that girl can't defend herself from such a beating," I said, looking at my sister with fury in my eyes.

"But it's also what Sirena wants. If you intervene, she'll report to the principal and, thanks to her high authority, you'll be both expelled and imprisoned with no chances of release."

Sirena's minions returned and took over what she was doing. This was going too far. With rage burning in my eyes, and my fists closed up tight, I couldn't bear to watch her suffer any longer. If I had allowed her to endure more of it, she would've died. I yanked my arm away from my sister and went over to them, ignoring Gabriella's warning.

"Hey!" I yelled, which caught the bullies' attention. "Leave her alone! She's already suffered enough!"

"*You* stay out of this, Bernard!" Sirena yelled, as she pointed at me. "Or are you planning on defending her over *me*?"

"What happened in middle school was not my fault! You brought this on yourself! It's bad enough having to fixate over me, but beating on students who haven't done anything is wrong?! You're a disgrace to your hall monitoring duty!"

"Look who's talking, Robin Fool!"

My eyes widened in disbelief, and she continued with a cruel smile, "And yes, I overheard the principal this morning, and unless you want to face expulsion and life imprisonment, you better not interfere with discipline!"

"You're not disciplining..." I pointed at her victim, "...*this* girl!" I looked back at Sirena with anger in my eyes. "You're abusing your position and her! It's illegal!"

"So is interfering with punishments given by law enforcement!"

"Along with blackmail, attempted murder, and eavesdropping on other people's business! Now, leave her alone, or face the consequences!"

Sirena walked over to me and responded mockingly, "Well, let me ask you one thing, Bernard! Who is Principal White going to believe, huh?!"

She pushed me backwards, which provoked my anger. If she wasn't going to leave her victim alone the easy way, then I would have to make her leave her alone the hard way. My eyes were glowing, and with mass concentration, a sonic boom shot from them. The hypnosis hit three of Sirena's minions, but she teleported to avoid it. She hadn't changed at all. That was the second time she'd dodged my power. She always made my power predictable. It was as if she'd trained herself to avoid powers that she deemed predictable. There was no other explanation. And at my command, I told them, "Leave that girl alone."

They did as I commanded, and I walked over to the poor, beaten girl. Before I could lend her a hand, my neck was grabbed roughly from behind. Sirena had teleported back. She threw me to the ground and pinned me down with her right knee. Choking me, she held my neck down with her left hand. Sirena made a right fist, and in a major fury, beat me to a bloody pulp. Her eyes burned with rage as her punches grew out of control, never giving me a chance to fight back. My nose bled. I wanted to cry from that much power with each blow, but at the same time, I wanted to get angry.

Everything somewhat blurred. Whether that was my punishment for calling her out about the past or for saving the girl's life, either way, I didn't want anyone around me to suffer. Deep in my mind, I was worried that if I died, everyone I knew and loved, and those who loved me in return, would suffer. But at that moment, a rock hit her in the back of her head. She turned around, unintentionally releasing me from her grip. I looked as well, and right before my eyes, I saw the girl, on her feet, levitating five more rocks with her right hand. Phoebe's eyes were fueled with so much rage. Earth Manipulation scared even the Teleporter Gang, who were trembling in fear. She aimed her right palm at Sirena.

"Do it again, Peyton, your back will be next!" The girl yelled.

"That's impossible!" Sirena screamed back as she stood up. "You can't possess more than one power! No one can!"

"Well, perhaps I can! Now, get out of my sight, and take your lackeys with you!"

Not wanting to anger the girl further, Sirena called back her minions and teleported away. It served her right for what she had done to the both of us. I saved her victim's life, and her victim saved mine. That made both of us even. Just as I was about to offer a handshake, wings appeared behind Phoebe's back, and the rocks dropped to the ground. It shocked the hell outta me. She was like an Angel. Before I could say anything, tears rolled down her cheeks, and she said, "I'm sorry. I should never have shown this to you."

The scared, winged girl flapped her wings and flew away, leaving me confused. What was her problem? Did I interfere with problems that she could've handled herself? Was it my criminal background? I did not know, and neither did my sister. But I had to intervene. Sirena and the Teleporter Gang would've killed Phoebe otherwise. As Gabriella and I walked back home, I kept pondering who that girl was. We could tell that she was more than a Flyer. Why did she have more than one power if a Tribe was suitable for only one? Why both a Flyer and an Element Manipulator?

There was only one person who could help me answer my questions, *if* he could answer them. That person would be the asshole I called my father. He was a lawyer and represented the accused and state theories, and critical thinking based on what the assigned accused did and didn't do. He was supposed to defend me as any other lawyer, but he only did that in public. After Mom died, he would abuse me without reason, making him the prosecutor as well. If anyone knew whether or not this girl was in trouble for possessing two powers, it would be him. I sighed in both resignation and self-defeat. There was no point in avoiding him any longer. I needed to have a chat with him ASAP.

VI- Kent Bernard

I still didn't like the idea of having a stepmother in the family. It was like Gabriella pointed out a day earlier, Hestia, who was in her dark-green gown with a blue headband and black high-heel shoes, was not as bad as I'd thought. She was kind, gentle, everything my mother used to be. She was even the owner of Hestia's Diner, ironically not founded by her, but owned by her nonetheless. Still, I had no intention of accepting her as a stepmother, which she understood right away. And she didn't even blame me for running away from home once, but, to my confusion, subtly agreed with me.

My father was reluctant to accept my decision of not accepting Hestia as my stepmother, but he wasn't always an asshole. Before my mother died, he was a good person with a sense of knowing the difference between right and wrong; thanks to her making certain he would always show respect for the right reason and keep his selfishness at bay. He was always respectful of the choices Gabriella and I made. But that wasn't possible anymore. Now, he was strict, unwilling to listen to reason.

At dinner, over chicken with carrots, peas, and corn and drinks, we gathered like a normal family. Gabriella and I had milk, Hestia had water, and my father had red wine. We said Grace before eating, which was traditional in our family from both sides. Too bad I was not allowed to feed Rosy some of my chicken like I used to. My mother had allowed it, limiting it to three pieces of chicken. When she died, my father forbade me from ever doing so again. And whenever I tried, he smacked my hand.

Now it was time for me to ask my father a question, which had been in my head for quite a while. After gaining some confidence I asked, "Is it possible for someone to possess more than one power?"

"Don't speak blasphemy at the dinner table, Kent," he answered sternly.

"I was just asking a…"

"I don't care what you're asking. Do not ask me that again."

"It was just a simple question."

"Come on, Jacob," said Hestia. "At least just answer his question. There's no harm in that."

My father was not happy about what I'd asked at first, and he put the fork down and glared at Hestia, upset with her for supporting me. Without any other alternative, he sighed in defeat and looked at me with a stern expression on his face. He finally answered, "Will you not talk about it anymore if I answer your question?"

"Yes, I promise," I said.

"Very well. Yes, it is possible for a Dúnamis to have more than one power, but it is heresy to have that. There are rumors going about the existence of those with more than one power, and it is the government's job to handle the crisis. If there was anyone with more than one power, the consequences would be severe."

"And what are they called?"

Dad was irritated and shouted in anger, "We made a deal, Kent! I said question, not questions! Now, zip it!"

His shouting startled me. Told ya my father lost the will to listen to reason. If he wasn't going to tell me what the individuals with more than one power were called, then I would have to figure it out on my own. But come to think of it, I'd noticed that girl manipulating rocks, which was the Earth Element, and extending her wings before flying away. How could she commit heresy if she'd saved my life from Sirena?

I didn't want to risk exposing the girl that had saved me. Instead, I decided to keep my mouth shut about the subject. No wonder he'd said my question was blasphemous. He didn't want to answer it from the start. As a character from *Harry Potter* once said, *"Curiosity is not a sin. But we should exercise caution with our curiosity."* In other words, I needed to be careful on who I asked for guidance, because the wrong person might be offended by certain questions.

But my curiosity was not completely satisfied, and it wouldn't be. Not until I'd found out what type of Dúnamis that girl was. If I didn't find out soon, I'd be unsatisfied for the rest of my life. There was definitely something worth knowing that the Nova Vegan government didn't want us to know about. So, to keep my father from knowing my intentions, I said I was full and asked to be excused.

I went to put my dishes away, but Hestia offered to do it, much to my astonishment and my father's irritation. Though I still hated the idea of having a stepmother, despite knowing she respected my feelings, my father expected me to respect his wishes and hers. Whatever, I would've said. But an ounce of sarcasm from me and he would not hesitate to punish me again. When I went to my room, Rosy followed. Since we were separated for three years, we needed to make up for lost time.

***

As Rosy kept me company, I went into my computer to find out about the multi-power individuals. Why was the subject of it labeled heresy? Why did my father not want me to know about them at first? What was the government hiding from the public? Using the internet, I sought out answers. If Phoebe was a heretic, she would never have saved me. She would have left me to die. And it was a good thing Dad didn't notice the bruises on my right cheek, let alone the left black-eye, thanks to my sister covering them with makeup after coming home.

After typing in "multi-powered individuals", I saw there was no information about it. That was not possible. There had to be some answers on the internet somewhere. I hadn't come this far to quit now. So, I kept looking through fourteen pages, until I found a term that I had never seen before- Pasdúnami. It was tempting, but I needed to know the truth. With one click, a bunch of articles popped up, containing a lot of information about the Pasdúnami. They were involved in the news, interviews, and various media.

One article shared an account of forty individuals with more than one power saving the world from the Global Cataclysm. And they were all Pasdúnami. The first and most important leader was known as Samuela Mentor, who foresaw the Global Cataclysm and led the thirty-nine other Pasdúnami to stop it. The second leader was Cedric Falco, who prevented the volcanoes from reaching the climax of eruption that would devastate every part of the planet, including the United States, Europe, and Africa. The third leader was Hironobu Mizuchi, who stopped mega tsunamis and reverted cyclones and whirlpools, saving many populated cities, such as Tokyo, Seoul, London, Washington D.C., and San Francisco. The fourth leader was Vivian Garcia, who healed those infected by plagues of any kind. The fifth leader was Bongani Chizoba, who manipulated the elements of the world and created artificial beings to protect everyone in Africa and the Middle East. The sixth and last leader was Alice Harris, who disguised herself as a corrupt politician and hypnotized corrupt politicians into helping people get to shelter. The politicians were also hypnotized into providing what they all needed to survive the cataclysm. Something looked familiar about this Samuela Mentor, but I couldn't put my finger on it. Was it just a coincidence, or was I missing something?

Anyway, the second article talked about a failed coup against the Nova Vegan government staged by the Pasdúnami. The war lasted for ten years with heavy casualties on both sides, ending with the Nova Vegan government as the victors. I guess some of the civilians were on the government's side, while the rest of those who sided with the Pasdúnami were either tortured to switch sides, banished from Nova Vega, or executed. It was in that year Nova Vega was born, and the coup started immediately after its birth. This was also the event where the Immortals and Time Travelers were labeled blasphemers.

There was a third article related to Pasdúnamis activity. It revolved around a little girl named Janice Campbell, who was thirteen years old at the time, on the day her parents were killed for their status as Pasdúnami by orders of the Chancellor of Nova Vega, Cyria Jelen. The whereabouts of the little girl from that day forth were currently unknown. But it was rumored that she had the ability to travel to different dimensions.

It seemed that I was mistaken. The Immortals were not the first to be labeled heretics after all. The first Dúnami to be labeled were the Pasdúnami, and the Nova Vegan government did a good job covering it up. Every detail revolving around the Pasdúnami had been erased from the archives of the internet, but they forgot about one more link. But as I said before, Phoebe couldn't be the enemy of Nova Vega, because she'd saved my life. I didn't care what she looked like on the outside.

I heard footsteps coming closer to the door, and so did Rosy, hence her barking, which I told her to shush. I didn't want my father to hear. I frantically closed out the articles regarding the Pasdúnami. Coming into the room, it wasn't my father, but Gabriella. Rosy, with her tail wagging excitedly, was happy to see her. My sister was happy to see her, too. But it was cut short when she gave me a stern glare. I was nervous at first, and I asked, "What?"

"You're a bad liar, you know," said Gabriella. "I knew you weren't full."

"I didn't want Dad to get suspicious."

"I know, but next time, lie better." She walked to my bed and sat down, with Rosy jumping up and sitting with her. "Ever since you came home, you lost Dad's trust. He knows what you're capable of. He fears that your ability to make choices of your own will be your downfall."

"Including choosing to protect a Pasdúnamis?"

Gabriella's eyes widened in surprise, and Rosy's ears stood straight up in bewilderment. It was their first time hearing that term. I explained to them what I'd read from the articles that I discovered online, the ones that the Nova Vegan government forgot to delete. If there was anyone that I could trust to keep Phoebe's status as a Pasdúnamis a secret, it would be my sister and our dog. Instead of reacting negatively, my sister stood up from my bed, walked over to me with Rosy at her side, and took my right hand.

"I believe you," she said. "It's only heresy if more than one power from one person is used for evil. That girl saved you. Now, we must do everything we can to protect her."

"But I never got her name," I said.

"Perhaps tomorrow you'll get the chance. Until then, let's make a vow."

We did our very own sibling vow of secrecy. We stood up and held our right hands in front of our faces with our fingers and thumb pointing upward. Gabriella went first and said, "I, Gabriella Tanesia Bernard, solemnly swear to keep the status of the girl who saved your life a secret from the public of Nova Vega and only share with those whom I can trust to keep it hidden from now until the day of my death. If word gets out, we, and the person and/or people in our protection, must stay in the dark until the commotion passes away and becomes forgotten."

"And I, Kent Tavi Bernard, will do the same. And from this moment on, I, with the help of those I trust, will protect the girl who saved my life and be there for her through good times and bad. Let this vow remain unbreakable until the day of our passing. May the Maker protect us all. Amen."

"Amen."

With the vow forged, we became the protectors of Phoebe Truman. Tomorrow, when I see her, we would officially introduce ourselves to one another. It was now a life debt that I would pay, and I knew that Gabriella would be able to help out as well. Tomorrow would be our first day as the protectors of our first Pasdúnamis.

VII- Phoebe Truman

I never meant to reveal myself as a Pasdúnamis that day, especially for the second time. I blamed myself for revealing my secret not just to Kent, but also to Sirena and the Teleporter Gang. How could I even give him a chance to show me gratitude when I was already aware that exposing myself in public meant death in Nova Vega? If word got out, the Nova Vegan Secret Police would take me away and end my life for what they viewed as heresy.

I wasn't from the Flyer Tribe as the public believed. In fact, I belonged in too many Tribes. Well, six Tribes, technically. The Flyer and Element Manipulator Tribes were two of the six. The Flyer Tribe was the ally to the Pasdúnamis Tribe for over a century, and it had kept its affiliation a secret for a long time. But my parents were still the leaders of the Flyer Tribe nonetheless; since they used that power more often than they did the others. I didn't feel like I belonged in any Tribe, expressing nothing but my own shame. By learning that the government saw the Pasdúnami as a threat, I took their words to heart in secret, living in constant fear of them because of my Tribe status. Sometimes, I even wished that I had never existed. Then again, had I not existed, Kent would be dead, or perhaps never interacted with Sirena that day.

***

I flew through my upstairs bedroom window like I did every day and placed my bag near my bed and the window. Falling face down on the bed, I heard a voice at my right saying to me, "Have you been bullied by Sirena again?"

"Go away, Ferenc," I muffled. "I'm not in the mood."

"Talking always helps."

"Not always."

"Phoebe, don't talk that way."

"Why not?!" I snapped, as I looked at my brother, who was sitting on my chair at my work desk. "Sirena is never gonna stop! I wish she would just leave me alone!"

Ferenc had a concerned expression on his face, and he stood up from my chair and walked over to me. He took my hand and noticed the dirt and dust. That's what happens when I manipulate the earth. He gave me a disbelieving look. I yanked my hand away and said, "I had to. After some boy saved me, she and the Teleporter Gang went after him. They were going to kill him, and I didn't know what to do."

"And you manipulated the earth?" he asked in a stern tone. "Phoebe Bridget Truman, exposing yourself as a Pasdúnamis is dangerous, and it can put your life at risk."

"What else was I supposed to do, let him die?"

"No, but he might not have either. He could've stood up for himself."

"But he didn't. He was losing his focus, and I had no other choice. Besides, Flyers can't fight."

"True, but..."

"But nothing! And after Sirena and the Teleporter Gang ran off, the boy I saved was trying to thank me. At least I thought he did. I never stuck around to find out."

"You made a wise decision to take precaution. For all we know, he could've been aware of our kind from the very beginning and would've turned you over to the Nova Vegan Secret Police."

He sat down on the edge of my bed. I was settling down for a moment, and to my surprise, my Siamese Cat Beatrice, or Beet as I called her, came out from under my bed and jumped on the bed between the both of us. Her eyes were ocean-blue, front paws cream-colored with back paws black, and some light-ginger on top of her head. I named her after one of the main protagonists of *Divergent*. My brother knew how crazy I was about the book series; I always cried in the end. So, the name for the cat he got me for my tenth birthday was his suggestion to me, which I took right away. She hopped into my lap, meowing, which was her way of letting me know that things would be okay. Ferenc placed his left hand on my right shoulder and told me the same thing.

But there was something that confused me. Where in NC State University did Sirena place my brother? I asked him that, and he answered, "The lockers. And don't worry. Nobody noticed me teleporting. And don't feel bad for what happened. What's done is done. It's time to put the past behind us," he said hugging me. "And I won't let anyone take you away, not even the secret police."

I hugged back and responded with a relieved, yet embarrassing smile on my face, "Thank you, Ferenc."

The next time I encounter Kent, I needed to be careful. Ferenc was right. For all I knew, he was loyal to the government and would turn me in. It was better to not take any chances.

VIII- Phoebe Truman

The second day of school should have been better than the first. The plan was for Ferenc to get me inside the school without being caught by Sirena. Encountering her on the first day of the new school year twice was enough. And after the incident with exposing myself as a Pasdúnamis, I hoped that she wouldn't mess with me anymore. So, instead of using teleportation, my brother snuck me through the window next to Mrs. Strickland's office. It was a good thing she hadn't arrive yet, otherwise, she would not be pleased.

Plus, I decided to skip my morning routine of watching the sunrise from the top of Goldsboro Water Tower. Ferenc knew a thing or two about telekinesis and used it without anyone looking. There was only an hour before school started anyway. We said goodbye to one another before he departed for NC State University via flight, and I sat at the same spot as yesterday, getting ready for the second day. Before that happened, I was ambushed. Someone yanked my hair and dragged me through out of my chair and straight to Mrs. Strickland's office. My face scrunched up in pain with my eyes closed in painful agony. I tried desperately to fight whoever had attacked me, but my attacker pulled harder, forcing me to let out a painful scream.

Before I had a chance to call for help, I was pinned down hard on the table, and in front of me were two black-cloaked people. They morphed into two male teenagers right before my eyes. The tall twin looked to be over six feet. He had dark hair, green eyes, and wore a brass sword pin on the black uniform's right side of the chest. He was the one responsible for yanking my hair earlier. The shorter, slightly chubby-chinned twin had the same hair color and uniform, except he had brown eyes, and the sword pin was on the left side.

"Word on the street is that you're a Pasdúnamis," said the short twin. "We were informed that you're not only a Flyer, but an Element Manipulator, too."

"And don't play dumb with us either," said the tall twin. "We're professionals in discipline." He yanked my hair again; which forced me to let out another painful scream, pinning me to the glass window next to the door I came through. He slapped me in the face with the back of his hand. "And there is a price to pay for possessing more than one power," he said, looking behind him at the short twin after releasing me, letting me fall on my knees. "Right, Cass?"

"Yes, Calvin." Cass walked over to me, grabbed the collar of my uniform gown, and forced me to look directly into his eyes, causing me to breathe heavily, my eyes to widen, and my heart to pound fast in fear. "It's a crime punishable by death."

He slapped me in the face as well and pinned me back down on the desk. They were staring down at me with cruel grins on their faces. I was already in a lot of pain from all the physical violence, and it was like a nightmare that became a reality, but I did my best not to cry, not to show any weakness. In their eyes, there was hatred, anger, and eagerness. Could they be the same people Seifer, Mark, and Valeda told me about? Could they be the Emmerich Brothers? I was too frightened to ask, which only pleased them more. Cass and Calvin were monsters in my eyes as if they were sent by the Devil to extract my soul and drag me to Hell against my will. They were worse than bullies. It was as though they were hired by the secret police to ambush me and assassinate me from where I stood.

Wait a minute! The Morpher brothers with so much brutality that they possess the capability to use any discipline and get away with murder! Oh, no! Seifer and the others were right! Cass and Calvin were definitely the Emmerich Brothers, and that was my first time encountering them! Sirena must've gone to them for help the previous day! There was no other explanation than that! My friends had warned me about them, and I was about to face their version of discipline!

I noticed Cass making a fist with his right hand, while his wicked grin widened, a chuckle forged underneath it. My eyes widened in fear. He was about to give me a deathly blow in the face. I shook my head, trying to signal them not to do it, but all it did was encourage them. The short twin wound his fist back, but before he could do anything, I sent my powers barreling through me, my eyes glowing like the sun. A sonic boom resonated from them, fear turning to rage due to the immediate danger.

My hypnosis hit both of them at the same time, causing them to zone out like drooling monkeys. I commanded Cass to let me go, and he did just that. I gave them a brilliant smile as an idea hit me. I stood up straight, and they walked backwards.

"I am not a Pasdúnamis," I said. "Sirena hallucinated, but she shall not be harmed. She didn't lie, but miscalculated. I, Phoebe Bridget Truman, am a Flyer from the Flyer Tribe along with the rest of my family, and nothing more. Now, move along and go to the library before homeroom starts."

The hypnosis process was complete, and they forgot about my status as a Pasdúnamis. To my relief, they left the art room. Going to the next building hrough the hallway and turning right, which was the direction to the library, the twins disappeared out of sight. Well, that went well. Thanks for the warning, Seifer, Mark, and Valeda.

"That was a nice comeback you did back at the office," said a familiar voice.

My eyes widened in fear and disbelief. I turned around slowly. I couldn't believe it. It was the same red-haired boy who had saved my life yesterday; Kent. He'd already noticed what I did, and without hesitation, I decided to hypnotize him into forgetting what he saw. But when my eyes glowed, so were his as he noticed what I was going to do to him. With the sonic boom, our hypnoses negated. And before I knew it, he'd teleported and reappeared behind me, covering my mouth before I had a chance to scream.

"Before you say anything, yes, I know what you are," he said. "But I'm *not* going to turn you over. If I was, I would end up no better than Sirena and the Emmerich Brothers combined. After reading about your kind yesterday, I noticed that the government itself is more messed up than it is now. Now, I'm going to let you go, but don't run away anymore. Alright?"

I nodded in agreement. I felt like I could trust him. I didn't know why, but there was something about him that stood out. And so, he released me, and I sat at my assigned desk. To my surprise, after he teleported, I discovered that Ferenc, my parents, and I weren't the only Pasdúnami. That boy was also a Pasdúnamis. I wondered if his family were Pasdúnami, too, or if he was the only one in the family. I wasn't sure. So, I asked him, "Who are you, and what Tribe are you from?"

"I'm Kent Bernard, and I come from the Hypnotist Tribe," he answered with an honest look, sitting on the desk near me.

"Then, why do you have teleportation powers?"

"Long story short, I've had it since I ran away from home."

My eyes widened in disbelief. He developed more powers during his days as a juvenile delinquent? Was he already aware of the existence of the Pasdúnami long before he did his research? What other powers did he possess? And who was the girl with Kent that day? His girlfriend? His sister? His cousin? Or just a friend? I wanted to ask him, but we were in a public classroom, so we needed to come up with a plan to discuss it privately.

"I'm Phoebe Truman," I said. "It's nice to meet you, Kent."

"Likewise," he responded, as we both shook each other's hands. "And if you're wondering about all of the questions in your head, let's go to the janitor's closet after second period."

What the hell?! I thought to myself, as my eyes widened in disbelief. Was he a Telepath, too? That's what I would like to know, too. He continued, "Janitors usually clean up the halls during lunch hours and after school anyway."

"Good idea."

"Well, I gotta get to homeroom." He got off the desk, walked to the door, and looked back at me with a confident smile on his face. "See you after second period."

I smiled, finding him a very caring person, someone I could depend on through thick and thin. I responded, "You, too."

Once Kent left the classroom, I finished up getting ready for the second day of school. The good news was that this week was a four-day school week. The bad news was that after this week, it would be five days a week, excluding holidays. The only problem was some of the festivities during holidays were banned around the same time fiction writing was banned. Halloween was illegal and branded heresy, Labor Day was a work day, Thanksgiving was banned, and Christmas was for celebrating the Birth of Christ and nothing more. I didn't blame Kent for going against strict laws made by the Nova Vegan government. Hopefully one day, things would be very different.

As he walked away in the same direction as the Emmerich Brothers, I knew that Kent and I would get along just fine. He saved me from Sirena and the Teleporter Gang after all. Then again, I would've done the same thing for him. And I had a feeling that we would have to watch each other's backs, just in case the government or the secret police found out about us.

See you at the janitor's closet, Kent.

IX- Kent Bernard

I was so glad that Phoebe was able to listen to reason freely and without hesitation back at the art classroom. The previous day outside of school did not end well, and I could tell that she was insecure about her status as a Pasdúnamis; hence her flying away out of what she believed to be shame. Being a Pasdúnamis was nothing to be ashamed of, unless you were around the Nova Vegan government of course. Who could blame her for trying to hide it from the public? Or perhaps she fled out of fear that I might be affiliated with the government, even though I wasn't. Either way, it was good to see that she didn't run away from me that time.

Then again, I would feel insecure, too, if the government found out I was a Pasdúnamis myself. But they didn't find out about it, because they didn't see me having more than one power. If my father found out about it, he would turn me in. He told me before that having more than one power was heresy. So, it was wise not to let him know about my powers, which, other than hypnosis, were telepathy, element manipulation, and teleportation.

You're probably wondering: why I didn't use teleportation to get away from the Morpher Police Officers from the very first chapter? Well, because I would end up exposing myself as a Pasdúnamis, and they would turn me over to the government. They would most likely torture me for information, which I wouldn't have since I wasn't even aware of their existence at the time, and kill me. Instead of exposing myself as a Pasdúnamis, I reluctantly let myself be arrested. So, as long as the public didn't know about my being a Pasdúnamis, it was all good. Until then, I would need to wait until after second period, where I had chemistry class, to meet with Phoebe at the janitor's closet.

***

The janitor wasn't around and there was still time before going to the cafeteria to have a chat. First things first, I had to look at both sides of the hallway to make sure no one was around, let alone watching. With the coast clear, I closed the door and turned on the light, relieved that it was just me and Phoebe. It wouldn't be nice to talk to someone in the dark, unless it was during bedtime. Weird, I know, but necessary to know who I was talking to.

"Okay, so far the only witnesses who are aware that you're a Pasdúnamis are Sirena and the Teleporter Gang, right?" I asked.

"So far, yes," Phoebe answered. "I just hope she didn't squeal on me to more than just the Emmerich Brothers."

"If she did, we'll just hypnotize them like you did the Emmerich Brothers."

"Sirena is smart and highly perceptive. She knows how to read people based on their powers. She's been doing that for years, studying them, observing them, and that includes the Hypnotist Tribe. The government would catch us before we get the chance."

"Trust me. I know how to handle the government. Being in the streets for three years has its advantages."

"Speaking of which, why were you in the streets for three years? I know people are not allowed to get jobs until after they graduate from college and all, but why did you run away from home?"

My eyes widened in shock when she asked me that. It was something I'd told only to my younger sister, but I didn't tell her the whole truth. After yesterday, I would have to let Gabriella know the whole truth later. For the time being, it was time to tell Phoebe the whole truth first. After all, my life hadn't been simple since my mother died. So, I think it was about time that I told her what happened before I ran away from home. I closed my eyes and calmed my nerves before opening them back up.

"Just keep it between the both of us and Gabriella, my younger sister. I'll introduce you to her later," I said. "And if you see Seifer and Mark, them, too."

"You know Seifer and Mark?"

"You kidding? We've known each other since kindergarten. But back to what I'm about to tell you. It all started during my childhood..."

X- Kent Bernard

Things were good and simple, even though Nova Vega had strict laws about almost everything, including holidays, in romance, the choice of careers, etc. And ever since I got *The Hunger Games* for my twelfth birthday, I wanted to be a fiction writer. But being part of the Hypnotist Tribe, the only careers I was allowed to go into was being a lawyer, a police officer, a detective, a counselor, a doctor, or a therapist. Plus, a published novelist career was banned for over a century.

My mother would want me to follow my dreams and not let the rules get in the way. My father would agree with her; before he became the strict man that I know him to be today. In fact, they always supported me through thick and thin alongside Gabriella. The other one who showed support for me was my dog Rosy. Yes, Phoebe, I named her after one of the characters from the very same book series I mentioned. Gabriella gave her to me on the same day. I was told that no matter what career I choose to pursue, I should never quit on my dreams. But one day, a tragedy happened.

***

I was thirteen, and it was a month after my birthday, as well as twenty-two days after Gabriella's tenth birthday. When we got home from school, we noticed that no one was greeting us. It was strange. My mother always greeted us. We dropped our bags and ran inside. When we got in, we noticed Mom on the floor with a bag of spilled groceries near her. We ran over to her in panic and shook her shoulder, attempting to wake her up, she was still not breathing. My sister went over to the phone, while I performed CPR after calming my nerves through three deep breaths. Twice it failed, but the third time worked. She got her breath back, and began to cry. She held her chest as if she was in pain. Gabriella managed to call the ambulance and after waiting for a few minutes, it arrived. We went with her to Wayne Memorial Hospital, the only place in the Forbidden Zone that didn't deny access. My father arrived after receiving a phone call from the hospital. But when he arrived, we got news that she only had six days to live due to a mysterious fatal illness, one in which there was no cure. Even the doctors weren't sure what it was. Hope was lost.

My father glared at me as if I was to blame for what had happened to my mother. How could he blame me if my sister and I saw our mother like that after coming home? Either he assumed that we weren't home fast enough, or he was letting his emotions get the better of him. Either way, he forbade us from ever seeing her without any reason.

One of my old teachers once told me that sometimes in life, whenever a lovebird is about to lose someone close to them, they feel as though they want to blame someone for something that isn't really their fault. Their emotions become unbearable and overwhelming, clouding and warping their minds as a result, thus making them lose their connection with reality.

After five days, I received a phone call from the hospital, asking, at Mom's instruction, that I should go see her and bring Gabriella along. And I did. It was unfair of our father to forbade us from seeing her, and it was the last day that we would see her alive.

***

We went to the fifth floor when we arrived at the hospital, room 517. As my sister and I entered the room, following the advice from the receptionist; we saw our mother. She was as pale as a ghost. Despite what she looked like, we were happy to see her, and she was the same way. Gabriella and I needed to be with our mother before she passed on. We sat by her side and held her hand, bringing a smile to her face.

"Does your father know you're here?" Mom asked.

Shaking my head, I answered, "No."

"Good. He wouldn't be pleased with you two coming anyway."

"How are the doctors treating you?" Gabriella asked.

"Like I'm prepared for a funeral, which I'll have soon." Her happiness turned to sadness as tears rolled down her eyes. "Listen, Kent, Abby, even if there was no cure, not even the Healers could do anything about it. And with the Returners gone, my time is almost over. But promise me one thing."

"Yes, anything," I said.

"Look after one another, and keep each other safe. And I'm sorry we never got to have more time together."

"It's not your fault."

"We didn't want you to die," said Gabriella, as we all shed tears.

"Neither do I, children," she said, as the three of us hugged in sadness. "Neither do I."

We spent the night with her in her room, and when morning came, she was gone. While I shed tears once more, I held Gabriella tight as she cried for our mother. I wanted to believe that it was all a dream and that she was still alive and all healed up, but I had to face reality. She passed away, and she was never coming back.

***

Our mother's funeral was held two days later, and Gabriella cried again, while I held her close into my arms. Seifer and Mark were with us that day. Uncle Rex and our cousin Riley were there, too. Riley had slightly tan skin, black hair, and hazel eyes. He usually wore a gray short-sleeve shirt with a black jacket over it, blue jeans, and black shoes during his free time, but he didn't at the funeral. Uncle Rex, on the other hand, had fair skin, blonde hair, hazel eyes, and usually wore a black business suit with a red tie and black shoes. Not everyone had the same strength of mind, especially with the appearances of people. Some people would be so focused on their grief that they would not pay attention to their surroundings, let alone their own well-being.

Unlike Riley, Uncle Rex showed no sign of sadness. He showed only anger, hence dragging our cousin out of the funeral against his will, refusing to let him pick even a single flower to put on Mom's grave. Yes, he was very abusive toward my cousin, for he had no compassion or kindness like Mom did. All he cared about was her inheritance, in which he took all for himself. I know it should've gone to Dad, but Uncle Rex, who had a complicated sibling relationship with Mom for years, threatened him and had no trust of any kind in him. Like my mother once told me, it was complicated, so I never understood what went on between them. And so, Dad gave Uncle Rex all of Mom's inheritance, since he believed that none of his former in-laws deserved it, nor did Gabriella or I.

But that wasn't the worst part of my side of the story. No, that day was only getting started.

After the funeral, my father met Hestia and started dating her right away, much to mine and Gabriella's dismay. Even she knew that it was too soon. He didn't care. He only dated Hestia just to get rid of the grief that struck him after Mom's death; his way of what he believed to be fate and, denying it to himself, filling the void in his heart. And when he did, he treated his grief like it was all but an illusion, a distant memory, a past that was never meant to exist. There's a difference between moving on and hiding grief. Dad was living a lie, and dating Hestia changed him, but not in a good way. It was in a selfish way.

***

On what should've been Mom's thirty-ninth birthday, my anger toward Dad continued, and he no longer cared about mine or my younger sister's well-being, let alone our feelings. Not to mention he had no intention in celebrating her birthday. But he called me and Gabriella into the living room. Smiling with joy, I presumed that he remembered her birthday, which made me very happy. But as my sister and I sat down on the couch, Dad announced that he and Hestia were "engaged to be married." We were dumbfounded as we stared at each other.

47

What? Mom's been dead for almost a whole year, and he's already decided to have a new wife? A person was supposed to be dating a lot longer than a year or less before getting married, but not my father. He wanted a new wife right away no matter how long he dated. Gabriella was happy about it. I wasn't. Deep in my mind, I was angry. I wasn't ready to have a stepmother, nor did I like the idea of having one. In fact, I never wanted a stepmother at all. I wanted my father back, the one from before Mom passed on.

***

Later at night, I made a decision to run away from home. I packed up my clothes, a pillow, a blanket, and stole some bread, jelly, creamy peanut butter, cereal packs, six bottles of milk, and six bottles of diet cola. I wasn't planning on returning to the place I once called home. After what Dad did, I viewed it as Hell, and away from it as Heaven. Rosy wanted to come along, but I told her that I didn't want her to. Instead, I told her to "watch over Gabriella." She was sad at first, but she accepted the task. I said goodbye to her and that I loved her. I felt bad leaving her since she wanted to come along. I was her owner, but my sister would have to be her owner now.

It was also sad that I would have to leave Gabriella. Unlike me, she felt happy having a new mother around the house, and I didn't want to take that away from her. I was disappointed in her, but at the same time, I didn't want to see her sad. I loved her too much to take that happiness away from her. I promised Mom that I would look after my sister, but I never said how I would look after her. It didn't matter. As long as Rosy was with my sister, I would always be there for Gabriella no matter how far I was going.

And so, I snuck from the window and closed it tight. Running far from the neighborhood and away from the house, where I lived when I was a baby. It was time for me to live on my own. There was no going back.

XI- Phoebe Truman

I had no idea that Kent had a rough life. If my father had behaved this way, I would feel the same. And the part about his cousin having an abusive father that only wanted Mrs. Bernard's money, that was even worse than being bullied by Sirena and the Emmerich Brothers combined. I felt sorry for him and terrible about what he had been through all those years. That, and I was angry at his father for putting him through hell like that.

After Kent told me his side of the story, I was interested to know how he got more than one power, but I noticed that I was supposed to meet up with Seifer, Mark, Valeda, and Asteria for lunch. Then, with my lips curling up in the form of a brilliant smile, I had an idea.

"Hey, Kent," I said.

"Yes, Phoebe?" Kent said.

"Do you want to sit with me and my friends at the cafeteria? Seifer and Mark will be there. After all, you haven't seen them in four years, right?"

Smiling, he responded, "Yeah, of course I'll sit with you guys. Do you mind if Gabriella comes along?"

"Not at all. The more the merrier."

***

Kent was happy to see Seifer and Mark again, and it was the first time he met Valeda and Asteria. Gabriella was a really nice person, and we became fast friends. Valeda, not easily fooled by the makeover powder, noticed Kent's black-eye and touched it. And just like that, his face was healed, and his black-eye was gone. She said she was "not a fan of people eating with injuries." She saw it as gross table manners among the Healer Tribe.

"So, my brother told me that you're a...you-know-what," said Gabriella.

"I am," I responded, smiling.

It was a good thing my friends were already aware that I was a Pasdúnamis, after keeping it a secret for a long time. Ferenc was pissed when he found out what I did, but he reluctantly let the whole thing slide. And they were trapped in the locker room in the small building at the back of the school; thanks to the

Teleporter Gang. Thankfully, Seifer managed to use his teleportation to get them out. And if Sirena and her minions did get to the Nova Vegan government, I knew that the Bernard Siblings would use their hypnosis to wipe their memories of what they witnessed.

And to our surprise, there was a boy that jumped out from behind Kent and Gabriella. The sudden jump startled Kent, and Gabriella shrieked. I was startled as well before I face-palmed in irritation. The boy chuckled from her shriek, much to her brother's annoyance, when he face-palmed. Two minds think alike.

"Damn it, Riley," he said, making me stand to attention. "You haven't changed a bit."

"Hey, we're not supposed to use *that* language on school grounds," said Asteria.

"She's right," said Gabriella. "Even before Nova Vega existed, profanity wasn't even allowed in high school during the Days of Old."

"Speaking of old," Kent glared at Riley, "shouldn't *you* be doing something else, besides surprising us?"

"Now that you mentioned it, yes," said Riley, taking something from his jacket. "Check this out."

He opened his hand and there was a striped newt. Its back was black-brown with orange parallel dorsal stripes, the underside was yellow with black spots, and the eyes the usual black. Gabriella opened her eyes wide while backing away a bit. She was freaked out by the sight of it. Mark and Valeda were amazed, much to Kent's annoyance. Seifer, on the other hand, said to Riley, "Dude, you're not supposed to bring pets to school, and newts are poisonous."

"Only if they're not treated carefully," Riley responded. "I found him and his brothers and sisters after their parents were killed by hunters during my trip to Georgia three years back. I named him Newt after the character from *The Maze Runner*."

"Ew, no one wants to see your newts, Riley," said Gabriella. "Bringing him and his siblings over to my house was bad enough. Plus, Rosy had to go to the vet to be cured of the toxins after she licked him. But bringing him to school?"

"Good thing I'm wearing gloves."

"Which you should wash along with your hands before eating and drinking. Now, get Newt away from me."

He did what she said, but not before putting his pet newt away. And Seifer was right. Bringing pets to school was a big *no-no*. And the cool thing was that the four of us had pets named after deceased heroes from dystopian media. Who said pet owners can't name their pets after fictional characters? Mark had a bald eagle named Cole, Seifer had a dove named Roy and a black and white cat named Henry, Valeda had a lizard named Diva, and Asteria had a black wolf named Tess, and a red and white Siberian Husky named Nova. It was like it was destiny that brought us together at this very moment, except when Riley came back from the restroom and sat next to Gabriella, much to her face-scrunching displeasure.

"So, I heard you're a Pa—."

Gabriella jumped, noticing her cousin about to blurt my status out loud. She managed to cover Riley's mouth before he could complete the word. It was too close for comfort. Kent looked around to see if anyone heard what was said. No one did, thank God. I would've been exposed otherwise, and not everyone in Nova Vega was open to the idea of a person being a Pasdúnamis.

"What?" Riley asked in a muffle.

"You almost squealed in a public school, dummy," Kent scolded subtly. "It's taboo territory in Nova Vega."

"Oh, sorry."

Riley blushed in embarrassment before Gabriella released his mouth. Yeah, he should be sorry. He would've had me arrested and executed for having more than one power. And how did he know that I was a Pasdúnamis? The Bernard Siblings asked him the same question, and he told them that he overheard Kent and me talking in the janitor's closet. Kent's and my eyes widened in disbelief. Even Gabriella was upset. Riley told them that no one else was around, and that he was very good at keeping secrets as well. The irony was that he almost spilled the beans, and I was glad he didn't.

Still, I felt insecure about my status, and Gabriella could tell something was wrong with me. She said, "Phoebe, there's nothing wrong with being what you are. You can't let that bother you."

"Yeah," said Riley, who was concerned alongside his cousins. "Why are you so against being a you-know-what anyway?"

"Well, if you must know, it's been that way since I was just a child," I answered, as I rolled my eyes in annoyance before looking back at the newt lover. "I was ten at the time, and it was the first time I had ever discovered what I was."

XII- Phoebe Truman

Before I moved to Goldsboro, I used to go to school at Pittsburgh. It was called Sunnyside, and Ferenc, my brother went to school there, too. I was known for keeping to myself, and had never been good with making friends. Being a Flyer, most people in different Tribes, such as the Morphers, Telekinesists, Animators, and Teleporters, would make fun of me, even call me cruel names and throw stones and stuff at me, calling me Pigeon Girl for example. Back then, I never understood that not everyone in those four Tribes were cruel and stereotypical. I tried my very best to ignore them, but every time I did so, they never stopped. The bullying was getting old to me, but never for them.

Then one day after school, I had an unexpected run-in with a gang of thugs known as the Animator Trio. Their names were Lex Dubry, Quint Coley, and Phil Milton. Lex was bulky with muscular arms and a belly with tan skin, a black Mohawk, a left yellow eye, and a large red scar through the other eye from the top of his forehead to his chin. Quint had muscular arms and legs, a beer-belly, pale skin, bald head, and light-blue eyes. Phil had a small belly and lacking muscles, but was taller than the other two by only a foot, and had light-brown skin, light-brown hair, and green eyes. They had been well-known for tormenting people for their own amusement. And they neither had a reason for messing with people, nor cared what they did to their victims. They did it for their own pleasure with nothing else better to do. The police never did anything to stop them since they were prejudice themselves. So, the victims of the Animator Trio would have to take matters into their own hands, whether to flee, or stand up to them.

While trying to do the former, an unexpected thing happened. The Animator Trio used their Animation Powers by aiming their hands at the rocks and trash cans, using their minds to merge together a gang of hybrid monsters made by the combination of the two. The rocks were created from the ground within the grass and the cement pavement. Tampering with dried cement parking lot pavement was a serious offense, which could lead to automobile incidents, resulting in either injuries, deaths, or both.

At the Trio's command, the Trash Rock Monsters shot me with multiple stones, treating me like an abused animal in the streets. My chest was in pain, deep cuts appeared like scratches on my arms, legs, and cheeks. I coughed up a small amount of blood when one large stone hit me in the stomach hard. The Trio laughed in a cruel manner, showing me no mercy. Tears of sadness and misery came from my eyes, mingling with the blood dripping from the gashing cuts on my cheeks. They were never going to stop, and I was about to die. Flying wouldn't do any good because my wings might get torn off if they were caught, which could lead to a Flyer's death through massive blood loss.

They went too far. I wailed with a mixture of sadness, anger, and fear. I screamed, "STOP!!!"

And just like that, the Trash Rock Monsters were immobilized, falling into pieces right before the Animator Trio's terrifying eyes. It was the first time I discovered I had more than one power. But they weren't the only witnesses. Dozens of children and several adults both in school and out, all of them stunned with disbelief, saw the whole thing. With anger fueling and burning in my eyes, I faced my frightened enemies and used my new power, Animation, to forge up the Mega Trash Rock Monster. My eyes were filled with tears, fueled by the deep hatred I'd developed toward the Animator Trio. Fear was implanted in them, and I was getting ready to end their lives through my creation.

Before I had the chance to do so, my parents arrived through their teleportation ability, sensing my danger via telepathy. My mother, Mary, had brown hair reaching the shoulders, hazel eyes, and wore a light-green gown with brown high-heel shoes. My father, Adam, had dark-brown hair, blue eyes, and wore a light-blue business suit with a white tie and black shoes. They rushed over to me and yelled at me to stop. I snapped out of my rage, and my mother held me tight. My father used Mass Hypnosis to make everyone, including the Animator Trio, who saw what I did, forget that I was a Pasdúnamis. He even made the cruel thugs forget what they did to me and what they were planning to do next. It didn't affect me and my mother, because my face was buried within her chest, and she had her eyes closed. Ferenc was there that day, and he shielded his eyes, too. My teary eyes changed from anger to guilt as I started crying for what I had done and almost did.

My mother, who was worried about me, extended her black wings and held me in her arms. My father extended his white wings and held Ferenc's hand before my brother, still stunned, extended his. We went back home to 430 Bastion Way, a blue house with a front porch and a garage at the back.

***

In my room upstairs, I was confronted by my parents who wanted to have a talk with me. I curled up like a ball. I didn't blame them. I was the one who almost got the Animator Trio killed. And what's worse, I even placed the whole school, including Ferenc in danger. Guilt was growing inside me, and my eyes watered in remorse. I asked them, "What's wrong with me? What am I?"

They were confused about what I said at first, but after looking at each other, they sat near me on the edge of my bed. My father looked at me, and I looked at him as tears continued to roll down from my eyes.

"What happened today was not your fault," he said. "Those teenagers were criminals."

"Your father is right," my mother said. "And there's nothing wrong with you. It's only natural with children your age. You've only begun to discover what you are. You are a Pasdúnamis, a Dúnamis who possesses more than one power, and as a Pasdúnamis, you must be careful when using more than one power."

"Using that in public is dangerous, and it frightens people. They're scared of something they don't understand."

"But I almost killed them!" I yelled, as I lashed out. "They wouldn't leave me alone! And as for having more than one power, if people were scared of me, then I shouldn't have been born at all!"

"Phoebe!"

"What?! They were thinking the same thing! People treat me different, especially since I'm a Flyer! Now, I'm nothing but a curse to them! Having more than one power for me is a curse! And reality brought me nothing but pain and misery!"

I buried by head in my knees and cried uncontrollably. My parents couldn't stand me looking this way. Then, my mother had an idea, and she embraced me.

Among the flock is a little bird,
Who is different within the raven herd,
For no one treated her with kindness,
And so, she fell into lonely sadness.

Then one day, she heard a voice.
It told her to rejoice,
And there's no shame for oneself,
"My child, be yourself."

I looked at my mother with curiosity, and then sang "God's Raven" along with her,

The little raven asked the voice, "Who are you?"
It answered, "I am the one who will help you pull through,
Just as Elijah was helped by my ravens,
Your ancestors who fed him at the valley haven.[1]*"*

---

[1] 1 Kings 17:2-6

Doubtful at first, the little raven went far away
To forge herself a new pathway,
But when she met the humans for the very first time,
They also treated her like slime.

She was about to lose all hope,
And there was nothing for her to cope,
But then, she met a lost young boy,
Who had recently lost all his joy.

Looking deep into his sad little eyes,
The little raven, much to her surprise,
Noticed that he was the same way as she,
And for the first time, light was at last free.
I smiled only a little, and my father sang along, too,
The little raven was born anew,
Her heart had ringed true,
The Maker made her into a girl,
Shining like a pearl.

The lost boy and the raven girl came together
By the will of their Maker,
Their differences brought them to their blessed happiness
And tamed their unhappiness.

I wiped my tears after the song ended, and we hugged one another as my sadness faded. My happiness returned when my parents reminded me that no matter how cruel reality may be, in the end there is always more good in it than bad. One has to be brave enough to confront and survive that cruelty. And that when things don't get better, even when walking away from it, I would have to stand up for myself and find the courage to confront my enemies, "but at the right place and the right time, as well as in the right way." What happened in the past was all in the past. The present is a gift from the Maker. My parents also told me to never be ashamed of whom I am and never view having more than one power as a curse, but instead as a gift.

Those were the words that stuck to me that day, renewing hope into my heart. But every day, it would only get harder and harder, even to move on. My parents were right. One day, I would have to make a stand. One day, I needed to find the courage to confront my fears and stand up to my enemies. And they told me to never let them have their way no matter what they do. And for that, I am grateful that Mom and Dad were there for me, whether they were near or far. Their words stayed with me through thick and thin. If Sirena or the Emmerich Brothers were ever to give me a hard time, I would be ready for them.

XIII- Kent Bernard

She did have a point. Avoiding the authorities was one thing, but standing up to bullies was more difficult, hence Sirena beating the crap out of me. And it was a good thing Gabriella covered Riley's mouth to prevent exposure about Phoebe's status. But I never had a chance to tell my sister about myself as a Pasdúnamis. It wasn't the right time to do so. Had I told her sooner, my father would find out, and he would have me arrested with no care of what outcome would befall me.

Good to know that my sister took great care of Rosy while I was away, even taking her to the vet after unexpectedly licking the toxins that resided in Riley's newts. That's one disease that the Healers can cure living beings from. The weird thing was that my cousin's newt was comfortable in his gloves, and he wasn't wearing them after coming out of the restroom.

"Hey, I was thinking," said Phoebe, looking at me with a smile on her face. "Kent, would you, Gabriella, and Riley like to come along with us to Hestia's Diner?"

"I can't," I answered after lowering my head with a frown.

Her eyes widened in a mixture of confusion and concern before asking, "Why not?"

"I'm grounded."

"Grounded?" Seifer asked, his eyebrow raised in curiosity. "For what?"

"Bank robbery, shoplifting, and running away from home."

"Hey, just because Aunt Fedora passed away..."

Provoked, feeling my eyes widened in rage, I interrupted Riley after slamming the table violently and shouting as I stood up, "Mom's death had nothing to do with me running away from home!"

Everyone in the cafeteria, including the staff, heard me, and Riley was startled. I was embarrassed when I noticed the whole room. Some were whispering, others were startled, and the rest only backed away. I calmly picked up my empty tray and stood up.

"I need to be alone," I said bitterly, as I walked away from the others.

***

It was only twenty minutes before third period, my history class, and I was reading my textbook to help me prepare for it and calm my nerves. I did feel bad about snapping at Riley like that, but people making assumptions about my reasons for running away made me mad. I already know the reason why I ran away three years back, and my cousin did not. *"Assumption makes an ass out of you and me,"* as my mother used to say. Not liking the idea of having a stepmother too soon was only part of the reason. The whole reason I'd left was because my father was self-centered and unreasonable, warped by grief and madness. It caused him to date and marry a random woman, and that wasn't right.

He stopped believing in miracles and love after he learned that she was literally dying health-wise, and he didn't even care, nor did he want to be around her anymore. Saying goodbye or farewell before the time actually came, along with premature funeral preparations before the outcome was determined, never sat well with me. He could've spent more time with her before she'd died. Instead, he rushed forward with his future plans. It was a good thing Gabriella and I disobeyed him. All that my mother wanted in the end was for her family to be by her side, and figuring that my sister and I were the only ones that came, it was more than enough for her. She wanted Riley to be there by her side, too. Unfortunately, she and Uncle Rex weren't on friendly terms with one another.

***

When I was eleven going on twelve, I once asked her, "Mom, how come Riley and his parents never visit us?"

She was wiping the dining room table before dinner at the time. But after asking her that question, she stopped and looked at me with a worried expression on her face. She answered, "What makes you ask that?"

I showed her an envelope addressed to her, and that I'd looked at the letter inside it. She walked over to me and grabbed it out of my hand, telling me "It's complicated." That meant that something was wrong between the two of them. And yet, she didn't want to talk about it. She told me not to look into her letter again, unless I had her permission.

***

The year before she died, she got a threatening letter from Uncle Rex, telling her that he would have her arrested if she ever contacted my cousin, her nephew, again. Like I said, he was very abusive toward Riley.

Speaking of mothers, after revealing that the reason for the relatives not visiting us was complicated, Mom told me that after Riley's third birthday, Uncle Rex filed for divorce. For what reason? We didn't know. Gabriella and I weren't even aware of Riley's existence, until we found response letters and photos in Mom's personal belongings. We first saw him at her funeral, but he never saw us, or even acknowledged our existence until about a month later. Annoying as he was during our real first meeting, he knew how to make us laugh at times, helping us get through even the most difficult situations. He was a frequent visitor, sneaking out of his house without Uncle Rex knowing about it. Not to mention that he skipped a grade when he was seven years old, putting him in the same grade level as my sister. But after Dad announced his engagement to Hestia, Riley stopped visiting us. I never saw him again until three years later.

I should never have yelled at him back at the cafeteria. Still, he should've thought about other people's feelings before his own. He was as much at fault as I was. I was the one who snapped at him for being insensitive about my feelings, but then again, I was not one to hurt other people's feelings when I felt pain. Being grounded for committing crimes for the right reasons and running away from home made me bitter.

Considering it was almost time for third period, I made the decision to wait until after school to apologize to my cousin Riley and tell him and the rest of the group, excluding Phoebe and Gabriella since they already knew, about my reason for running away from home. Good plan, Kent.

***

After school, I met up with Phoebe, Gabriella, and Riley at the front of the school. Walking along with them, I apologized to my cousin for my behavior and told him my reason for running away from home. As we stopped near the fire station, he smiled and looked at me. "No worries, Kent." His smile faded. "And I'm sorry, too. I should never have been insensitive back there. Also," he smiled again, "Gabriella already told me."

"She did?" I said, as I looked at Gabriella.

"I did," she said. "Beat ya right to it."

"Hell, yeah, you did," I smiled, feeling sheepish.

"And I thought my old man was a dick," said Riley, as his smile turned into grimace. "I can't believe Uncle Jacob would do something *that* stupid, making decisions too quickly without thinking first."

"He didn't know better," said Gabriella, scowling sternly. "And who could blame Kent for running away. Sure, it was stupid to run away. Plus, I had to pretend I was happy just to stay on his good side, and show respect. And yet, Hestia already saw right through us. Even she played along."

"Why didn't she say no?" Phoebe asked.

"Because he would've threatened suicide otherwise until he got his way. Even if he was bluffing, he was being dead serious about getting his way."

"Guilt trip?"

"Guilt trip," Gabriella and I answered in unison.

"Point taken. Anyway," she said looking at me. "Kent, how were you able to get to the twelfth grade if you were a runaway?"

"Homeschooled myself, and I had help before I was on my own again. It's a long story."

Confused, Phoebe asked, "Help? What kind of help?"

"Another runaway."

Gabriella looked at me, blinking in shock, which made me blush. Despite my embarrassment, I didn't blame her. I'd never explained further. Apart from my status as a Pasdúnamis, I had to keep more of my history as a runaway to myself. And with no one around to hear us, it was safe for me to explain further, as we continued walking.

"Sis, Cuz, there is something you should know about me during my time as a runaway. Something I haven't told anyone else but Phoebe."

"Kent, relax," said Riley. "You can tell us anything. We're not like Uncle Jacob or my old man."

"If it's something related to what Phoebe has been experiencing, it's best to keep it to ourselves until we go somewhere secret," said Gabriella, as we met up with Seifer, Mark, Valeda, Asteria, and Ferenc at a stop sign.

Ferenc was not happy to see me when we first met. I read his mind and his thought; *Why did Seifer have to drag me into this?* He looked directly at me. *For all we know,* this *boy is in league with the government.*

"First of all, I'm not in league with the Nova Vegan government," I responded in irritation, much to Ferenc's surprise. "Second of all, if Phoebe hadn't saved my life and vice versa yesterday, neither one of us would be here."

"Don't be melodramatic! You could've defended yourself!"

"I'm not being melodramatic! I'm telling you the truth!"

"*You* were the reason why my sister almost got exposed as a Pa—!"

"STOP IT!!!" Gabriella shouted, startling us. "Let's agree to disagree," she looked at me. "*You*, stop proving Ferenc right," she said, looking at Ferenc. "*You*, don't make an ass out of yourself to Kent," she said looking at both of us. "And I can see that you both want to protect Phoebe from the government. I get that, but fighting about who's right and who's wrong will not solve anything. The only way to do this is to work together, and to make sure *she* controls her emotions when using her powers without getting publicly caught."

I felt ashamed about the situation, and that was the first time I'd seen Gabriella scolding someone. But my younger sister did make an excellent point there. Fighting about what the truth is would only complicate the task at hand. Phoebe's protection was our top priority, and for the time being, the government viewed the status of Pasdúnamis as heresy and a threat to Nova Vegan Society. Even if we were to prove otherwise, some people would believe us, but the rest wouldn't.

"We should have a name for the group," said Riley, much to our confusion.

"Wow. That was random, Mon," said Mark.

"A group name?" I asked.

"Yeah," Riley continued, as he smiled. "I was thinking that we should call ourselves the Aurora."

"Why?"

"Well, this is a new experience for us, and things are changing around us every day. And no matter how dark and grim things get, we will find a way to overcome them and look on the bright side, like the borealis of the night sky up north. Phoebe having more than one power…"

"Along with me," said Ferenc.

"Yeah, and we're there to protect her. Think about it, guys. A person having more than one power may not be such a bad thing. Wouldn't it be better to be loved by society instead of being feared? We could inspire people, even free society from harsh rules."

"Riley, you're crazy," I said doubtfully.

"Maybe, but even the old can blend with the new. Students can have part-time jobs again, the world can be rebuilt, the environment can come back fully and completely, and the United States can be reborn."

"Not a bad idea, Weston!" said a sarcastic, yet familiar voice, leaving us stunned with fear.

We looked at the source of the voice, and to our dismay, it was Sirena again. But the Teleporter Gang was not around. Instead, there was the Emmerich Brothers— Cass and Calvin. This was not our day. Then, Sirena continued without her sarcastic tone, "But that's not going to happen. As long as the government runs the country, you nine won't be doing anything."

"And by the way, Truman, thanks for exposing yourself as a heretic to us in the art teacher's office," said Cass, as he and Calvin took a case of contact lenses from their jackets, much to our horror.

"We were prepared, too," said Calvin before he and his brother put their contact lens cases away. "We didn't train in a cadet military academy for nothing. As I said before, there's a price to pay for having more than one power," he held out his hand. "Now, come quietly."

I stood in front of Phoebe to shield her. "If she refuses?"

"Glad you asked," Sirena answered, as she held her own right hand and snapped her fingers once.

From inside the fire station to the ditch at our left, there were people in black armor and helmets with red shoulder plates. One of them had a dark mask and a gray cape, indicating he was the leader. There were more of them behind the building and on the roof as well. They surrounded the nine of us and had us at gunpoint. We were all afraid as we huddled close together.

"You summoned the secret police?" Ferenc scolded.

"Silence, heathen!" said the Captain of the Nova Vegan Secret Police. "For coddling a Pasdúnamis and interfering with the Law Enforcers of Nova Vega, all eight of you are hereby under arrest," he looked at Phoebe and pointed at her saying, "and *this* girl will be tried and condemned for heresy."

The eight of us surrounded Phoebe, putting her behind us to be her shields. Our enemies threatened to have her taken away and killed. We chose to die rather than go quietly and surrender. Mark used his animation ability. He mixed the concrete and ripped it from the stone bricks next to the grass. The materials merged together to form a man-like structured army with the wooden hands morphing into guns equipped with stone bullets. Asteria morphed into one of the secret police officers. The rest of us stood our ground to ready ourselves.

But Sirena burst out laughing alongside the Emmerich Brothers. The nine of us were confused, yet at the same time, nervous.

"Have you learned nothing from yesterday, Bernard?" said Sirena. "I'm a Teleporter, remember? And I'm a quick study."

She teleported inside the surrounding circle, seized Phoebe, who yelled in fear, then Sirena teleported outside of the circle. We were caught off-guard. Since he was a Teleporter as well, Seifer, who was furious at the stunt Sirena pulled, teleported in front of her in his attempt to save our friend, but one of the officers took out an electrical baton and stunned him. The other officers placed Seifer and Phoebe in power-proof handcuffs. Another officer stunned Asteria and handcuffed her also after she was forced to morph back into her real form. The Telekinesis Secret Police Officer stunned the rest of us, while Phoebe was placed against the wall, being prepped for the firing squad.

Students and school staff that hadn't left school grounds witnessed the whole thing. Even Mrs. Strickland, who covered her mouth in shock, Mr. Bayne; with a gaping mouth, and Principal White; who was raving mad at what he witnessed. And just as the secret police officers readied and aimed their rifles at Phoebe, Ferenc— desperate to save his sister— broke free of the telekinetic freeze with his own telekinesis and teleported to her, pushing her out of the way; taking the shots as a result. A majority of the school screamed in horror, and Phoebe went along with the students.

Deep in my mind, my rage grew from what we had witnessed. My brain screamed like mad as I struggled to break free with no success. The secret police worked to get Phoebe back against the blood-covered wall. She was going to be next in death. I didn't want to bear the thought of her feeling the pain of the bullets, which would bring a quick, painless death. I couldn't stand it. She was about to die. Sirena and the Emmerich Brothers showed no sign of pity or remorse, and I was about to scream. And just when the officers readied and aimed again, I let out a huge scream as my mouth unexpectedly unfroze.

"NOOOOOOOOOOOOOOOO!!!!!!!!!!!!!!!!!!!!!!!!!!!!" I screamed.

Then, the guns started shaking, and the officers were shaking along with them. My immense wailing levitated the guns, and they fused with one another like molecular atoms. My body freed itself, and I reached out my right arm as I ran in front of Phoebe. The morphing metal went to my hand, and it became a silver sword with a full brown hilt, all metallic.

The Aurora was freed from the telekinetic freezing process as well. Did I develop the ability of telekinesis? How was that even possible? Was it my devotion to save Phoebe that brought about this new power? I wasn't the only one stunned. The Aurora, the Nova Vegan Secret Police, Sirena, the Emmerich Brothers, and those left at the school were stunned. My status as a Pasdúnamis, the very secret that I wanted to reveal to Gabriella, Riley, and the rest of the Aurora, was exposed.

XIV- Kent Bernard

Three years earlier- After running away from home, I'd planned to start my new life in the streets. But as I reached Goldsboro Water Tower, I felt like I had forgotten about something. Wait a minute.

Oh crap! I thought. *My school stuff! I forgot about my school stuff! But I can't go back now! I have come so far!*

This was not a good sign for me. How the hell was I supposed to learn now?! If I didn't learn, I'd end up falling behind education-wise! Then, the unexpected happened. One minute I was at Goldsboro Water Tower, and the next, I ended up on top of what was left of the tall glass building in Boston. What was happening to me? How was that possible? There was no way I could have more than one power. I was stunned and scared at the same time. Next thing I knew, as my fear continued to grow, I was next to the remains of the Washington Monument. It was getting out of control. I appeared in random places that I couldn't keep track of, let alone control. And when it finally stopped, I was back in my room, but there was no one in the house; I was all alone.

I didn't want to take any chances of getting outside the room. Rosy would notice, and I would eventually get caught. Then, I spotted my ninth grade supplies and placed them in my bag. Before I had a chance to take my eraser, I was back at Goldsboro Water Tower. This was getting way out of hand. I was literally freaking out, and there I was, on top of the high school.

"Stop! Stop!!" I yelled, as I appeared from the top of the school to the top of Fort Pitt Bridge in Pittsburgh.

From Fort Pitt Bridge, I appeared at the junkyard across the street from 105 E. Holly Street. I shouted, "Why won't I stop appearing from one place to another?!"

"Because your frustration is getting the best of you!" said a voice.

My eyes widened in shock. I wasn't alone. I turned around, and there was a preteen girl with brownish-red hair, curling around her greenish-blue eyes. Her fair skin seemed lighter in the purple shirt she wore. There was a tear below the breast level of her shirt, her jeans were worn-out; exposing only her entire right eg an inch below her calf, and part of her left leg three inches below her knees. Her white tennis shoes had soot at the toe parts. Her right wrist was covered in bandages like a wristband, and her cheeks had soot markings as if she was ready for battle.

In her left hand was an empty can, which she placed inside a black plastic bag she carried. To my amazement, she was just like me. She, too, was a runaway. This was something I figured out after she asked me, "You ran away, too?"

"You, too?" I asked.

"Yep. But it's not safe out here. Daily patrols are on their way," she said walking through a hole in the fence. "Come on."

No point in arguing, I followed her lead. Without noticing, I stopped teleporting randomly. She was right. Perhaps I'd calmed my nerves without realizing it. That, and she did have a point about the Nova Vegan Police of the North Carolinian Branch patrolling the streets until 9 a.m. every morning. That's when they kept a lookout for anyone violating curfew during the middle of the night. Curfew in Nova Vega took place from 7 p.m. to 7 a.m. Anyone without proper authorizations or permission forms during those hours would be arrested and prosecuted. The punishment: A week in prison. Repeated offense: 1 to 3 years without parole.

***

The inside of 105 E. Holly Street was a huge warehouse, with a security system installed at the front of the massive room. It had everything from security cameras to ejection catapults to tranquilizer guns to cages. Behind the front of the warehouse were dozens of rooms, all of them empty, excluding the lights, desks, drawers, and beds. There was a kitchen and a dining room at the very back of the warehouse.

The place that used to be the loading dock was used as a large bathroom with twelve showers, twelve sinks, and twelve toilets, all of which were in their own stalls. The bathroom itself extended from the entrance to what was left of the parking lot. There was only one light at the very center of the ceiling, and the wall was recently made with bricks stuck together with cement. At each side of the wall were powerful hand and hair dryers.

And there was the hallway with a huge room. The room had a gray wall, a large electronics desk, a bed next to the huge window, a refrigerator, a private bathroom, a massive bookcase, and a small work desk. The girl that I met showed me around the room and said, "Welcome to the Former Holly Street Warehouse, my home away from Hell."

Nice way of saying an isolated place away from the unfair laws of Nova Vega. And perhaps the place away from my uncaring father. I could get used to it. The only problem was I didn't want to get myself too comfortable. It was her home after all. That was until she said, "And I see that you brought your stuff, including your school stuff."

I was stunned, and I asked, "How the hell did you know that?"

"Hey, only use *that* word as a name of a place," her expression turned from happy to stern upon hearing me cuss. "Maybe keeping obscenities at a minimum doesn't apply to some people," she twirled her right index finger before pointing at herself, "but it applies to the rest of *us*," she put her hand down. "So, don't use it too much around me. Alright?"

"Sorry. I didn't know."

"Well, now you do. And to answer the question you asked earlier, I saw your reaction before you teleported away. Believe me, I've seen first-time Teleporters having that reaction before. It was hard for them to control that power. And I don't blame you. We runaways can't always do whatever we want. We all need education ourselves. How else will we learn if we're not at school?"

"Exactly. And besides, getting jobs before being college graduates is against the law. Well, in Nova Vega anyway."

"Good point. But we also need to survive if we don't have family support."

"Isn't stealing against the law, too?"

"Dude, in this world today, you either steal, or starve, but only as a runaway under college graduate level," said the female runaway.

"And how are we supposed to learn new stuff and get to new grades without going to school? We don't even know about homeschooling."

"Maybe *you* don't, but I do. I'll tell you what. I'll homeschool you as I'll homeschool myself…" She held a ninth grade textbook related to Algebra, "…and you help me with stealing for survival."

I looked inside my bag, feeling my eyes widen in disbelief. Looking back at her, I saw that the female runaway stole my Algebra textbook for ninth grade. Smirking cleverly, I thought to myself, *She's good.*

Smiling, I held out my right hand to accept her offer. She smiled back, and we shook hands. My smile faded as I said, "Just for the record, I'm a Hypnotist. But I never had more than one power before."

"Does it matter?" she asked. "Do you realize how awesome it is to have more than one power? That's even better."

We stopped shaking hands, and she continued, "And since you're a Hypnotist by default, I can also teach you how to use your new teleportation ability without any worries."

"Thank you," I said. "I'm Kent. Kent Bernard."

"I am Cali Ross of the Teleporter Tribe. Welcome home, Kent."

XV- Phoebe Truman

Present- Ferenc, my brother, died to save my life. But I was next in line to be executed. I'm sorry, Ferenc. I shouldn't have exposed myself as a Pasdúnamis in the first place. I should've been more careful. It was too late for apologies. No more running. No more hiding. Only death.

The firing squad readied arms. This was it. There was no escape. It was the end of the line for me, just like Ferenc. My enemies aimed at me, my lips curled, and I closed my eyes after my body froze in fear. I didn't want to die, but there was no other way out. My death was approaching.

Then, there was wailing and the sound of materials fusing, splashing, fizzling, crackling, and freezing. I opened my eyes and Kent stood right in front of me with what looked like a sword. Hypnosis, teleportation, telepathy, and element manipulation, but how did he get in front of me if he was frozen with the Aurora? Unless, of course, he'd gained a new power; telekinesis, hence cancelling the effect.

He didn't just reveal his status as a Pasdúnamis to the Aurora; he also revealed it to our enemies and the people still in the school. Even Kent was stunned to notice that he could materialize a sword. He gripped it tight with both hands and looked at me.

"Are you alright?" he asked.

"Yes," I answered.

"Good," he looked back at the secret police with his new sword gripped in his hands while they armed themselves in sword-like batons. "One thing to know about enemies; never let them have their way!"

"Infidel!" yelled the Captain of the Nova Vegan Secret Police, as he looked at his officers. "Kill him!"

They charged at Kent first, and he stood his ground. Gripping his sword tight, he managed to block any attack thrown at him and cut down four of the officers across the chest. Seeing that he had the courage to defy the corrupt government, hope was given to me for the first time. I reached my hand out to the draining blood coming from the corpse of my brother. Mixing it with air, I materialized a dagger with a clear crystal blade. It was as though my brother's spirit was guiding me, as the weapon I forged telekinetically was made into the instrument of his revenge.

I ran to the secret police's captain and fought against him after he took out his own sword-like baton. Kent struck down two more of the officers as he slashed their throats. The corpses fell hard on concrete while I cracked part of the captain's mask with the blade. Nothing broken, let alone falling apart, except there was a crack from top to bottom at the left side of the mask's front side. His anger provoked, the captain slashed me across my shoulder, causing me to scream loudly in pain before I shook it off to clash my dagger with his baton-like sword once more. Blood dripped onto the concrete. My school uniform was torn and staining rapidly and my eyes were burning with rage. He grabbed my right arm, and I did the same to him, preventing each other from making a deathly blow. We wrestled one another, attempting to gain the upper hand, and Kent backed me up after he stole another officer's gun. He shot my opponent in the chest.

"Batter up!" he yelled, as he knocked the captain away from me with the hilt of his sword.

The hard whack cracked the mask further causing another piece to fall from it, revealing a left hazel eye. Then, I had an idea. We needed to remove the mask to find out who the Captain of the Nova Vegan Secret Police was. Either that or we would need to crack it completely. I dashed to him and grabbed hold of the mask, but he gripped me tightly, ready to stab me in the side. Luckily, Kent stabbed him in both arms to disarm him and force him to release me from his grip. And just when he was about to swing the hilt again, a voice shouted, "ENOUGH!!!"

We turned around and saw Riley being held hostage by Sirena. She had been given a gun by one of the surviving officers. Gabriella and Seifer were held captive by Cass and Calvin and Mark, Valeda, and Asteria were held against their will at gunpoint by three more of the surviving officers of the secret police. Sirena yelled, "Drop your weapons, or we'll blow your friends' brains out, literally!"

Not wanting to see our friends share the same fate, I dropped my dagger first, which dissolved back into blood and air. Kent went along, and the sword dematerialized back into guns. Sirena smiled deviously and said to us, "Now, put your hands behind your heads, and we will spare your friends' lives. Be glad the captain and I are merciful, unlike the Emmerich Brothers."

"Hey!" Cass yelled offensively. "I resent that remark! If anyone is more merciless, it's Calvin!"

"Excuse me?!" Calvin yelled, as he poked his index finger hard on his brother's chest, much to the latter's irritation. "If I recall correctly, *you* were the one who wanted to end Truman's life! Have you forgotten your training back at the academy?!"

"Shut up, dumbass!" he pointed at himself with pride. "I knew what I was doing!"

"Punishing criminals is our job, yes," he spread his arms wide and aggressively, "but using the art teacher's office as an execution spot is not right!"

Cass gave an arrogant smile and responded mockingly, "But we're not in the academy anymore!"

"Shut up!" Sirena yelled, startling the Emmerich Brothers. "No wonder the academy transferred you both here! You won't stop fighting and arguing!"

While the trio was too busy arguing among themselves, Kent and I exchanged confusing expressions before noticing, with a jolt, fire mysteriously appearing on Calvin's ass. Everyone seemed oblivious to what was happening to him until the argument stopped. Sirena and Cass sniffed the burning and noticed it. Calvin was confused, and the captain was about to shoot Kent, believing he manipulated fire out of nothing. How could Kent have done it if he was confused about its mysterious appearance as well? The gun levitated by itself and knocked the captain out, much to my surprise.

Calvin screamed in terror before running around like a maniac, unintentionally releasing Seifer from his clutches. Cass ran after him trying to put the fire out, which caused him to free Gabriella. Sirena was not pleased with the Emmerich Brothers, and Riley managed to hypnotize her without her noticing, commanding her to let him go, which she did. While the short twin chased the tall twin, he ended up with an unexplained atomic wedgie. And right before our very eyes, Gabriella twirled and swirled her arms, spinning her body at the same time. She materialized from the mixture of air and concrete, three bows and a couple of arrows, with only two of the bows levitating from the ground; she used only one. It looked like Kent wasn't the only Pasdúnamis in the family after all.

She, along with the two levitating bows, shot the three officers' armed hands, causing them to drop their guns and freeing three of my friends. Eyes widened in surprise, Kent and I walked over to her, and she looked at us with a smile on her face after lowering her bow.

"But how?" Kent asked.

"*You're* not the only one with this kind of secret," Gabriella answered. "Hestia knew, too, even before you did your research. Element manipulation manifested in me a week after you ran away from home. She kept it a secret, even from Dad."

"Then..."

She nodded and responded, "Hestia's a Pasdúnamis, too. She trained me in secret, told me that there's more out there than we think. They're not as rare as we originally believed after all."

"And I don't think you guys should've done that," said Riley, as he pointed at the school.

We looked, and noticed we had too many shocked witnesses on our hands. They acted as though they had never seen Pasdúnami before. Kent, not wanting to be viewed as a threat by his peers, walked over to the front of the school. Gabriella and I went along with him. His eyes were burning with courage, pride, and determination.

"People of Rosewood High!" he said, raising his rematerialized sword. "Everything that the government told you was a lie! Every law they made, any Tribe they condemned, they only use fear, deception, manipulation, and cruelty to control all of Nova Vega! It's been like that for over a century, since its foundation! Society suffered because of it! High schoolers and college undergraduates being denied jobs until they reach college graduate level because of strict Tribe Job descriptions alone, obsession with Tribe Purity, even taking away the will to think for ourselves based on Tribe restrictions, as well as limiting our freedom! If you all think for one second that the Nova Vegan government will ever treat us fairly, then you believe in a lie! After over a century, we're still its slaves and prisoners! In reality, the Pasdúnami were never the threat! They were the solution! Whatever the reason, they knew what Nova Vega's government had done, and we all have to fight back to get the answers we need!

"But we do know *this*: The Pasdúnami rebelled against it, because it enforced laws that were the same as many other dictators had done before it!" he pointed at Ferenc's corpse near the back of the fire department. "*This* is the result of what the government has done and what they plan to do to all of us if we think for ourselves! The people of Nova Vega shouldn't be afraid of their government! It is the other way around, because they let power warp their minds!" Kent looked up at the top of the flagpole, presuming there was a surveillance camera at the orb. "Government of Nova Vega, I know you're watching this, like you have everywhere else in the country throughout the years; from public stores to schools to convention centers, and to most of our homes! You can bribe us, torture us, banish us, and even murder us without mercy, but we will never submit to fear anymore! Fear and respect are *not* the same thing! We, the people of Nova Vega, don't serve you! It's YOU that need *us*! You brought this battle on yourselves, allowing power and authority to corrupt your hearts, becoming the very people you fear the most! You should fear us, but in the end, you ought to fear *yourselves*! Pride in being feared will become your downfall! If we die, *you* die with us!"

Those still in the school were talking among themselves, trying to understand if we could be trusted. Before they had a chance to make a final decision, Kent was grabbed from behind by the Captain of the Nova Vegan Secret Police who held him at gunpoint. Mrs. Strickland's look was that of horror and disbelief. Principal White came out from the building and yelled, "Let Mr. Bernard go, Captain!"

"You're not in a position to make negotiations!" snarled the captain, as his exposed eye glared at his frozen hostage. "*This* boy will die for defiance and heresy! Unless, you want to die with him."

"Don't listen to him, Principal White!" Kent answered. "You said that the Morpher Officer that arrested me was your brother, right?! If that's true, then weren't you in the streets, too?!"

"Shut up!"

"No, Mr. Bernard is right!" said Principal White, who morphed into his younger self, revealing the ragged pants and a dirty gray shirt with a hole in it and a missing right sleeve. "I was one of the homeless along with my brother and his friend," he morphed back to normal. "The government was going to have the three of us exiled after our families lost their jobs over increased taxes; until one of the Seers saw our future and our place in Nova Vega. With our parents gone, she raised us until we were old enough to have careers of our own. Now, I see why Kent went into juvenile delinquency. And it would explain the children and the lower-class families being saved from banishment according to the newspaper; hence building homes for themselves and finding jobs of their own, supporting families and children, providing needs and education for generations to come."

That revelation left me amazed, as well as touched. Kent didn't just steal to survive. He also provided for the homeless when the government wouldn't. His principal was visibly upset with what his true enemies had done and what they were planning to do. God knows the homeless didn't deserve to be cast out. It was survival for the Nova Vegan government and those affiliated with them, and death for the rest, survival of the fittest.

Glaring malevolently, the captain responded, "Until we caught him and finished what we started!"

"Then, Kent was right to defy you!" Principal White looked at Gabriella with determination and defiance. "Ms. Bernard, now!"

Gabriella used her telekinesis to give the bow and arrows to Principal White, and he shot at the captain's right hand. But something happened. The arrow stopped midway, and the captain released Kent, putting his hand out. The arrow itself morphed into a gun, and the captain revealed himself to be a Pasdúnamis, much to everyone's shock. My eyes widened as I felt the outrage and disbelief. Talk about hypocrisy right there. He used telekinesis and element manipulation at the same time.

Principal White attempted to shoot the captain again, but was shot in both hands, getting disarmed in the process. He screamed in agony and the captain angrily levitated him into the air, as if crucifying him. Sirena, looked painfully at the suspended principal before looking at the captain in anger. Then she went over to the latter and yelled, "You're one of them?!"

"Yes, I am," The captain answered calmly. "But sometimes you have to fight fire with fire. Even Pasdúnami can be of some use to the government. However, the rest are unworthy and chose defiance. And here's the example for it."

He shot Principal White six times in the chest. Desperate and horrified, the Aurora and I rushed over and attempted to stop the captain, but he used his telekinesis to stop and freeze us, even preventing us from cancelling the effect using his mind. He even made sure Seifer and Valeda wouldn't reach the principal in time by having his officers stun them. Not even Riley or Mark was prevented from sharing that fate. We cried out and pleaded with our enemy to stop and let the principal go.

Then, the captain, whether ignoring our pleas or enjoying our unbearable, emotional torment placed the gun on the ground, aimed the palm of his right hand, and gripped the same hand tight, causing Principal White to vomit blood violently; some of it dripping from his eyes. To our horror, as Mrs. Strickland and dozens of the students screamed in terror, we noticed that the captain used his telekinesis to crush Principal White's heart into oblivion. The corpse fell on the ground, and the captain looked at the entire school.

"Let this be a lesson to all of you!" he yelled aggressively. "Anyone who defies the government will face punishment through death!"

After witnessing what had transpired, after what they heard from Kent earlier, after being raised on what they were expected to believe; bitterness, rage, even defiance was seen in their eyes for the first time in years. Finally, they saw who the true enemy was. No longer would they have to live in the shadows of the tyrannical government, nor be slaves under laws based on prejudice, extreme supremacy, and inhumanity.

The first to rebel was Mrs. Strickland who materialized a gun from the brick wall in the hallway and aimed it at the captain. "Then, you'll have to kill me next!"

"And me!" said Mr. Bayne, as he used telekinesis to steal the captain's gun.

The entire school of every Tribe chose to defy the Nova Vegan Secret Police, and Mr. Bayne managed to cancel the telekinetic freezing process, freeing me and the Aurora as well. Mark made twenty man-like structures out of concrete, dirt and grass. Weapons for them were made out of wood from the fence line. Asteria, morphed into Principal White, picked up the baton from one of the corpses of the secret police officers. Seifer teleported himself, Mark, Valeda, Principal White-Asteria, as well as the Grass-Covered Concrete Soldiers behind us, to face the captain and the secret police before looking at me and Kent.

"You and the Aurora take Ferenc's body and get out of here," he said, taking the last bow and arrows from Gabriella. "We'll handle the secret police and its captain."

"Where will we go?" I asked.

"I'm sure you and Kent can think of something. Just get out of the school."

"He's right," said Kent, as he used telekinesis to levitate my brother's body. "Let's get the hell out of here."

Feeling overwhelmed, I looked at the huge battle taking place at the school. My brother was killed, our school principal had his heart crushed, and now I was to leave my friends behind to go with the Aurora. And to make things confusing, Ferenc's corpse was coming with us, but for what reason? What was Kent planning?

With no time to argue, nodding, I answered with a worried expression, "Okay."

Kent, Gabriella, Riley, and I, along with Ferenc's corpse, ran through the army and passed the Emmerich Brothers. We turned to escape the upcoming battle, but not before Riley stole the gun from the secret police officer's corpse. There was no turning back for us.

***

Going to the first intersection and turning left before continuing straight at the T intersection, we encountered more secret police officers, who managed to catch up to us at the second intersection, blocking our path. Gabriella rematerialized her bow and arrow with air and shot some of them. Riley did the same with the gun. I extended my wings before materializing a dagger with bark from one of the trees and cut the secret police officers down from the midair. Kent kicked one of them off a hover motorcycle, and he got Riley to climb to the back of it. I sheathed the dagger in my pocket and carried Gabriella off the ground, giving her the advantage of shooting our enemies from above as I flew. Riley did the same thing. It was a high-speed chase between us and the secret police. According to what Kent told us during the road battle, we had to make certain that the corpse didn't get damaged. What was his plan anyway?

There was no time to answer, and turning right at the same intersection upon arrival was the wise decision. Out of fear, we didn't want them to know where my brother and I lived regardless of the surveillance cameras, hence avoiding them before entering the house. With each right shot to the engines, the hover police cars exploded on impact as the arrows morphed with explosives. Two or three of the officers, perplexed and terrified, flew off the hover motorcycles as the wheels were shot, either crashing into trees or buildings, or landing on the cars, causing them to spin out of control and crash into the ditch on either side. Some of them even flew off the other side of the highway bridges, falling into the deep ditch.

The secret police were very persistent. Giving up was never their forte. Then I noticed Kent reaching his hand out, and to our surprise, another highway bridge shook and broke apart along with the first bridge. The cars from both highway bridges either backed out of the way or drove away as the bridges landed in front of our enemies. At least the civilians were safe, and the Aurora and I managed to evade the Nova Vegan Secret Police.

***

We stopped right in front of the abandoned warehouse- 105 E. Holly Street. I had no clue as to why Kent would want to stop there. It must've been important to him. He got off the hover motorcycle and walked over to the entrance of the warehouse with Ferenc's body still telekinetically floating in midair. Confusing Riley and Gabriella and making me curious, I asked Kent, "Is that where you went after you ran away from home?"

"Yes," he answered, stopping midway to look at us. "This is also where my friend lives. She can revive Ferenc from the dead."

We looked at each other with a mixture of disbelief and surprise. A Returner living in 105 E. Holly Street? Now, that was something we didn't know about. I originally thought there was none left in Nova Vega. Some believed that the few that were in hiding were long dead. Gabriella walked over to her brother.

"Is she a Pasdúnamis, too?" she asked.

"Yes, Sis, she is. Any friend of mine is a friend of hers. That's her motto," he answered.

"Are you sure she can revive the dead?" I asked.

"Of course. She brought back several homeless children that were shot dead by the secret police once. If she can do that, she can bring Ferenc back to life. Come on."

With tears of joy, I realized I was going to see Ferenc again. For a moment there, I thought that my brother was beyond help. But now, I realized there is still hope for Nova Vega yet.

Ferenc, we're not ready to let you go just yet. God knows you didn't deserve to die, and with the help of Kent's friend, He'll send you back to the World of the Living. See you soon.

XVI- Phoebe Truman

Thanksgiving five years earlier- It was my eleventh birthday, and my brother and I had some surprising news from our parents; we were planning to move to Goldsboro! That was amazing news. At last, a place where I could actually make some new friends without having to be afraid of being nervous around them. Well, at least in my opinion anyway. Ferenc, on the other hand, never wanted to move, because he had some friends in Pittsburgh. But knowing him, he would get used to the new place eventually.

***

While my parents prepared a Thanksgiving/Birthday meal the day before the move, I flew over to the roof and top floor of the David L. Lawrence Convention Center. I sneaked there all the time to get some peace and quiet. It's one of places where Ferenc wouldn't find me, let alone scare the crap out of me. The space on the roof was the shape of a T, except the horizontal line was shorter than the vertical line. Considering the building had been abandoned for centuries and the plants on both sides had died out.

On the other hand, the view of the Allegheny River and the bridges known as the Three Sisters always gave me a calm feeling through my body. There were several buildings at the other side of the three yellow bridges, yet the middle and left ones collapsed during the war, leaving only the right bridge intact without any thought of rebuilding the others, as the government found it a waste of budget. That was irritating considering how cheap and greedy they could be.

A breeze blew my gray, red, and blue striped scarf like a flag, while I stood at the front middle of the rails. But there was only one problem when it came to weather in Nova Vega. The government created a device that made certain it would be warm and sunny every day, even every season: The Weather Manipulator. Snow was not allowed out of fear that it would disrupt the crops growing in farms and gardens. Rain was fine, as long as it wasn't too much; hence the dead garden at the convention center. Same for the wind, including the blow I felt while on top of the convention center.

Thunderstorms, hurricanes, tropical storms, blizzards, tornadoes, etc., brought only death, destruction, and disaster. That part I understood, but keeping them out was not easy. Why would the government attempt to stop the weather from coming to Nova Vega when there was really no stopping it? It was simple. The weather, which came temporarily, or didn't come at all, ended up occurring outside the wall. The wall itself was like a shield, determining the climate and weather conditions. Survival is good, but what about everyone around the world? People don't always survive natural disasters, let alone escape. Apart from diseases, illnesses, disabilities, and more, the weather and natural disasters were known for being unpredictable. It wouldn't be fair for only Nova Vega to survive or escape them. Unfortunately, it was what it was. Nothing could ever be undone.

Before the wind artificially died down, I caught a leaf blowing right in front of me. It was the only one I caught. Where did it come from? Was it alone, or did the other leaves get blown away and never returned? What was it doing coming to the roof? It was beautiful and as bright as a crystal when the sun shone on it; a rare amber color. I always loved it when the wind blew and the leaf floated in the air. Looking back at the river, an idea popped into my head. I held the leaf with my left hand and reached my right hand out to the river, manipulating parts of its water, commanding it to come to me. I created a water sphere and placed the leaf on top of it. Levitating it was fun, until I heard a thought saying, *We found a Pasdúnamis.*

Dropping the water ball with the leaf on top, I looked to the river with one of the telescopes after putting a quarter I found on the ground in the slot. There was a boat of four officers from the Nova Vegan Secret Police. They had been hunting for Pasdúnami for years; with the government attempting to cover up the Tribe's existence, making it look as though they never existed. If anyone ever spoke about them, it was blasphemy as well. One of the officers had a sniper and he aimed directly it at me. I took a step back. Thinking fast, I extended my wings and flew away to the city streets to avoid incoming bullets.

***

Flying through Fort Pitt Bridge over the Monongahela River, there was one other place I would go to if I encountered danger— Emerald View Park. The location was Olympia Park Hike and great when avoiding bullies, but not the secret police. Their helmets were equipped with tracker scanners to hunt down criminals and fugitives of the law. Not even hiding behind the brick wall would help. For all I knew, they would end up surrounding me.

Looking at the other side of the wall, I saw the same officers coming for me. My heart pounded rapidly, sweat poured down from my forehead, and I was too petrified to even move a muscle. Then, I felt someone grab my right shoulder. I got ready to scream, but another hand covered my mouth. I struggled to get free. My screams were nothing but muffles, and there was a voice.

"Keep quiet, Phoebe, or the secret police will find and kill you," it said.

Turning my head slightly saw Ferenc. I hugged him tight, relieved that it was him and not another secret police officer. He shoved me a little and told me to wait, while he "handled these guys." And he did. He materialized two swords from the mixture of the bark from two trees and ten leaves each. The blades were green, while the hilts were brown. Every time one of the officers attempted to shoot my brother, he would teleport to dodge. One of the bullets almost hit me in the right shoulder, but it missed as I heard it whiz past my ear. When I looked behind me, I saw that it went through a tree and into another behind me. Keeping my mouth covered to prevent getting caught, I was glad not to have gotten myself killed.

Ferenc slit the first officer's throat, but he got tackled by the second, knocking them behind a rock. There was a scream from behind the rook so I didn't know what happened. When I walked over there, the officer was covered in blood. I thought he'd killed my brother. He told the last two officers that he knew where I was hiding, and my stomach dropped in fear. I hid behind the tree again. This was it. I was going to die. That idiot brother of mine had to go on a suicidal battle and get killed for nothing!

Then, I heard loud gunshots, blade-slashing and the sounds of blood-splattering, coming from my right; far from Ferenc's last stand behind the rock. Coming out of hiding, I walked over to where the sound was. Before I could, however, my eyes widened as I noticed a dead body in uniform. How was that possible? *I just saw him coming out! He murdered my brother.*

Someone grabbed my shoulder, startling me and causing me to jump. Turning around, it was Ferenc, and he was still alive. How did he escape death? Looking at him, I noticed two heads with their mouths hanging open, almost making me vomit at the sight.

Unbelievable! My brother morphed into one of them behind another tree after stabbing that officer in the heart. Based on the gunshots earlier, he managed to dodge more bullets after catching both of the officers off-guard, and before decapitating them. Pissed at him, I punched him a lot in the chest, calling him an idiot for scaring me like that. Two swords were dematerialized after I told Ferenc never to frighten me like that again, a promise he had no intention of keeping.

"Come on," he said, reaching out his right hand and extending his wings. "Let's go home before more show up."

"Right," I answered after I calmed down and took his hand, extending my wings.

We flew high in the sky and went back home just in time for the Thanksgiving and Birthday Dinner. I was glad to know that he made it out alive to make it for that occasion. If something bad ever happened to him, I wouldn't know what to do. I learned that day that I needed to be careful when using more than one power in public.

XVII- Kent Bernard

Present- It's been six days since I moved from the old warehouse. Well, Cali's home away from Hell according to her, technically. Things were difficult after moving there thanks to getting caught at the abandoned community college and grounded for a month. It was good to be back though, as it was a relief to see my second home. Any place was better than the home I viewed as my portion of Hell. Although things were about to get rough after I knocked on the door three times, especially bringing a dead body telekinetically.

Cali, armed with a shotgun, opened the door and aimed it at my face. I was shocked, and my friend, sister, and cousin were stunned. Ferenc's corpse fell on the ground after I lost concentration, which Cali noticed after hearing a loud thud behind me. She looked back at me, placed the shotgun down, and said with a smile on her face, "Good to see you, Kent!" she hugged me tight. "How have you been?!"

"Busy, Cali," I answered.

She stopped hugging and looked at the corpse, raising an eyebrow. "What's with the dead body?"

"That's why we came. We need your help in bringing…" I looked at Phoebe, "…*her* brother back from the dead."

Cali looked at her before looking back at the corpse. She gave me a stern glare, crossing her arms over her chest. "What happened?"

"He got himself killed to save his sister," I answered. "He saved her from execution after her status as a Pasdúnamis was exposed."

Her eyes widened in shock before uncrossing her arms and responding, "And what happened before you arrived?"

"W-W-Well…uh," I stuttered nervously. "I sort of s-s-s-started a rebellion before another one of our allies got killed by the Captain of the Nova Vegan Secret Police."

"And you didn't bother to bring that corpse as well?!"

"There was not enough time, and after discovering that I can use telekinesis, I can only levitate one body. Besides, you once told me that you can't revive the dead if the body was missing or in pieces," I said.

Calming down, Cali responded, "That's true." She looked at Phoebe again. "And since *she's* related to the person that once resided in the newly-fresh corpse, I'll see what I can do."

"Thank you," Phoebe responded with a smile on her face. "I owe you for this."

"Oh!" she smiled modestly. "There's no need to do that."

"No, Cali. I insist. In fact, I have something for you in return."

"Oh?"

She nodded and took off her backpack before reaching inside it. She pulled from her bag her book set of *The Divergent Series*. Cali's eyes widened in astonishment and excitement upon seeing it, and I could tell by the smile on her face, she wanted it. In fact, she's a big fan of literature that's related to dystopia. Not only were they entertaining to her, but they also taught her how to make the world a better place; and dreaming of preventing an even worse future.

Phoebe gave it to Cali, who took it, gazing down at the set, her eyes wide. She looked at her and said, "Thank you. You didn't have to, but I appreciate it." Cali looked at us. "Now, let's get the corpse inside, and I will begin the resurrection process immediately."

***

Being a Returner is not an easy task. There are several requirements that need to be met before resurrecting the dead. If neither of them is met, the person who died cannot be resurrected.

1) The body must remain in one piece. If in pieces, stitch it back up completely. Don't worry about the organs. They'll get recharged and restored after the resurrection process. Once the body is revived, the stitches will disappear, and the body will be in one piece again, never to fall apart.

2) The body must never be decomposed to air for more than a week, or month, depending on its condition.

3) The body must NOT be cremated. Even if the ashes stayed together, the resurrection process would be rendered a dud.

4) The body must be preserved for ten years or less depending on whether or not it gets buried. Any more than that would make the resurrection process useless.

In one of the empty rooms, Cali spent thirty minutes using her power to bring Ferenc back to life, her hands glowing throughout the process. She was on her chair near the right side of the bed with the corpse. Her hands were on the body's chest near the location of the heart.

While waiting, leaning into the doorway, I reflected on what had happened after we escaped from the school. What had become of Seifer, Mark, Valeda, and

Asteria? What about the students and staff faculty of the school? And how would Officer White react to finding out his brother was killed? There was no telling what the outcome of the battle would be, but I had to guess that it was getting bloody and brutal. The principal's brother would most likely blame me for it because of my criminal records. Inside my head, I was both pissed and afraid at the same time. The Captain of the Nova Vegan Secret Police killed Principal White. We could've saved him, but our enemy didn't want us to save him, seeing it as attempting to intervene with the execution. Until the commotion die down, we would have to lay low, pray that our friends and allies stay alive.

Phoebe paced around the middle of the room. I watched and worried about her while she hoped the resurrection process would succeed, or she would never see her brother. That much, I can tell from the edgy back and forth walking. I had to calm her down for Cali to concentrate. Like I said, reviving the dead was not an easy task for a Returner. It took time, concentration, and patience.

Riley, who sat near the doorway, pulled Newt from his pocket to pet him. Gabriella sat patiently with her legs crossed watching the resurrection process; until she saw Newt, then she shrieked and glared sternly at our cousin. Noticing Riley caressing his newt after hearing my sister, Cali pointed out the bathroom to him, reminding him to wash his gloves and hands before regaining her concentration. She wouldn't mind having an animal, reptile, mammal, etc. around in her home, since dystopia inspired her to help with the environment as well.

Cali's hands glowed bright. Soon the room was illuminated like a floodlight. Phoebe, Gabriella, and I covered our eyes with our hands. It was too bright for us to see. Cali, however, closed her eyes before her hands stopped glowing. With the glow gone, and my friend removing her hands from the chest, we uncovered our eyes to see what would happen. The bullet wounds on his chest were gone. However, Ferenc didn't open his eyes, let alone wake up. We were hoping that he would breathe. So, we waited, but nothing happened, and Phoebe, with tears in her eyes, fell on her knees and covered her face, her chest heaving with sobs. Gabriella and I walked over to her, getting on both knees, and holding her shoulders to show comfort. Cali, however, lowered her head, and I could see the look of failure on her face. She had never failed the resurrection process before.

But all of a sudden, the four of us heard gasping and heavy breathing, startling us as we looked to the source of the breathing. To our surprise, Ferenc was back, and was gasping for air as he sat up. Phoebe stood and ran to him, hugging him tightly. Ferenc had a confused look on his face. Tears fell from his eyes, and the eldest brother, with a smile on his face, embraced his younger sister, bringing smiles to our faces, too, as they were together again. Riley, upon returning from the bathroom, witnessed it as well, and he was overjoyed to see the Truman Siblings together again. It was a relief indeed.

After over an hour of death, Phoebe's brother was back and all thanks to Cali. But after exposing myself to the Nova Vegan government, and pondering, I realized what I'd done. And with the school rebelling against it, chances were all of Nova Vega could rebel against it. My mind was swirling with panic and horror. I wasn't ready for this kind of responsibility. The Aurora and I weren't ready for a rebellion. We needed to leave the country.

Standing up along with my younger sister, I walked over to Cali, Phoebe and Ferenc. They stood looking at me curiously, and I said, "We have to leave Nova Vega."

Phoebe's eyes widened in disbelief as she asked, "What? Why?"

"We drew too much attention to ourselves. Now the government will be looking for us, and we started a rebellion."

"Kent is right," said Ferenc, catching our attention. "When I was in the Invisible World, I heard the Maker's voice. He told me that my time in the Material World wasn't finished," he said getting off the bed slowly, then standing up cautiously, still recovering from the resurrection process. "He also told me that there's a threat that's much bigger than the Nova Vegan government itself. We don't know what it is, but we have to leave the country. The time for battle will have to wait another day."

"What about our pets?" Riley asked, as he walked through the doorway to join us.

"Hestia!" said Gabriella, snapping her fingers at our cousin, suddenly realizing something. "She's good with animals, and she has a place where she can watch over them."

"Where would that be?"

"She never said, but I trust her."

I didn't want to agree with the idea. Just because she married Dad did not mean I would have to be nice to her. Like I said before, she was a constant reminder of my father's selfishness. I walked to the doorway and stood there with my arms crossed.

Then, I heard Gabriella say in a worried, yet desperate tone, "Kent, I know you're still angry over it, and I respect the fact that you despise having a stepmother, and Hestia doesn't expect you to acknowledge her as such, but just give her at least one chance."

I lowered my head, still feeling frustrated. I wasn't sure what to believe anymore. On the other hand, Dad may have forced her into a relationship, so what other choice did I have?

Turning around to face my sister, I responded like a stubborn mule, "Alright, Sis, but only because she wasn't given a choice in the first place. After this, I never want to see her again."

"Kent!" Riley reprimanded.

"No, Cousin," Gabriella said, raising her hand at him. "He has every right not to want anything to do with her," she placed her hand down and continued. "Besides, she reminds him of Dad's selfishness," she looked back at me. "But, Kent, if you find it in your heart not to hate her, that's more than enough for her."

Rolling my eyes, I uncrossed my arms and responded, "Fine. I won't hate her even if I see her again for the last time. Before we get our pets somewhere safe, we have to get our stuff first."

"The only problem is I only have one power," said Riley.

"Nope," said Ferenc. "The Maker also told me that *you* have more than one power."

Gabriella and I weren't the only ones stunned by that revelation. Riley was shocked about it, too. Ferenc told him that the only abilities that Riley possessed other than hypnosis was element manipulation, teleportation, heal, and animation. He was also told that he would gain two more in the future. Riley didn't seem to believe Ferenc. If he could use more than one power, why hadn't he use them before? Were they still dormant, like the two future powers that have yet-to-come? Or had he not tried before? Either way, if his father knew about it, he would either turn him in or kill him himself. It was time to go to the Bernard Residence; but my sister and I couldn't go there alone.

So, I looked at our cousin and said, "Riley," I caught his attention, even though he was still upset with me for my stubbornness. "Come with me and Gabriella. We're going to need someone to look out for Dad while we're packing our stuff."

"Are you shitting me?!" Riley exclaimed.

"Hey!" Cali scolded. "Language, dude!"

"She doesn't like obscenity," I said.

"Oh," he said, blushing. "My bad!" he looked back at me. "Are you roaring me?!"

"Wow! Haven't heard that one in a while. No, I'm cereal. Someone needs to keep an eye out on Dad. We don't want to get caught."

"He's right," said Gabriella. "Now, let's get home and pack our stuff before Dad gets home, if he isn't already."

"I'll be on the lookout for the secret police until you three return," said Ferenc.

"Alright," I said, looking at Cali. "Watch over Phoebe and Ferenc. Their stuff will be next after ours. We don't want to put them at risk again."

"You can count on me, Kent," she said. "If the bad guys show up, my traps will take care of them."

As we placed our hands together, Gabriella, Riley, and I were teleported from Cali's home to the Bernard Residence.

***

83

Once outside the house, I opened my bedroom window— the fastest way to get inside the house, and the same way I sneaked out the night after Dad announced his engagement to Hestia. I didn't use teleportation because surveillance cameras might be anywhere in the neighborhood, and I'd already been exposed as a Pasdúnamis. The neighborhood would be put at risk if I was caught.

It was a good thing Dad didn't notice us coming inside the house. He wasn't inside. I gave my sister and cousin a boost through the window then grabbed my hands to help me in. We needed to pack our things fast, including books for entertainment and educational purposes, food, clothes, drinks, sleeping supplies, and medicine.

Riley was keeping an eye out for Dad from the front door. But while Gabriella and I were getting out some chicken from the freezer, much to our disbelief, we were caught. Dad held Riley by the shoulders and dragged him to the kitchen where my sister and I were at. Gabriella and I froze in terror when we saw him. Riley looked like a scared little boy, eyes barely closed and mouth quivering in fear.

"What did I say about visitors in this house?!" our father yelled.

"That's Riley, your nephew from Mom's side," I said.

"Well, your mother is not here anymore! And with her gone, *this* boy is no nephew of mine!"

Dad threw him hard across the floor in front of us. Riley was groaning in pain upon impact and could barely stand up on his own. That was cold. My sister and I looked down at Riley, concerned for him. I glared at our father in anger. And how did Dad get home so soon? Did it have something to do with the school fighting against the secret police, or was it because he still didn't trust me?

"What happened at school today?!" he yelled.

"It was just a bit of a misunderstanding," Riley answered, still attempting to stand up on his own.

"Don't bother denying it! I got a call from the police station! Several students, a few teachers, and even the principal at your school are dead!"

We didn't show any sign of emotions, because we knew how Dad would react if we did. Regardless of keeping what happened back at school to ourselves, he already suspected that nothing was right. We already knew that Principal White was dead, because we were there when that happened, but we didn't know about the other students and teachers. We were hoping that Seifer, Mark, Valeda, Asteria, Mrs. Strickland, Mr. Bayne, and the others were alright; we were beginning to fear for their lives.

After a long silent pause, Dad said, "Very well! If you won't talk willingly, then I'll make you talk!" he looked at Riley. "And I'll start with *you*!"

He was about to hypnotize my cousin Riley into telling the truth, but with fast thinking, I used my hypnosis to negate his. Dad's eyes widened in rage. And what was about to happen would leave him stunned.

"You stay out of this, Kent! Or I'll get the truth out of you instead!"

"No, you won't!" yelled Gabriella, as she turned on the water from the sink.

Reaching out her hand, she materialized the running water into a bow and arrow and aimed it directly at our father. He lifted his eyebrows, eyes wide, and stared in disbelief. Gabriella came out as a Pasdúnamis to him and said, "Now, you know what happened at school, Dad. The rebellion has begun."

XVIII- Kent Bernard

Two-and-a-half years earlier- For over six months, we stole to survive. Stuff like food, clothes, drinks, and even money. But whenever we received a visit from lower-class citizens and the homeless that escaped the government's wrath, whether through loss of families, job losses, or moving from one hiding place to another to evade them, Cali and I would give what we stole to them. They needed it a lot more than we did.

By providing for all their needs, we both built a new and better community for them, to give them a future for themselves. They were in the same boat after all. It was better than seeing them banished to the ruined wastelands that was once called the United States and the world. We even provided shelter in case something happened to their old shelter; whether it was patrols, the secret police, or bounty hunters, which happened on rare occasions.

Some of the members of the lower class were Healers, so there was no need for the medicine. No one would starve, or thirst, or fall ill, or die. The abandoned warehouse was their home, our shelter to them. And in the middle of the night, Cali and I shoplifted without getting caught by security cameras. No one in Nova Vega would take money from outlaws, due to the country being under surveillance. Because of that, if they recognized what we were doing, they would attempt to turn us in regardless. If we wanted to give them money without being seen as outlaws, Cali and I would need to have a clever plan. Like Robin Hood and Little John from the legends, we stole from the rich and gave to the poor.

***

On my sixteenth birthday; a year, five months, a week, and two days later, Cali got me eleventh grade textbooks to help me with my studies. But she and I weren't the only ones. Even the lower class needed education, and we even got help from adults that had lost their jobs as educators. And with the lower class becoming part of society after leaving the warehouse, new lower-class citizens came. It wasn't much, but we managed to help them out. They helped us in return for our services. But the day after my sixteenth birthday, Cali and I noticed that there weren't enough clothes for the new residents.

So, we both teleported to the clothes store called KTReynold Clothing and Footwear located at Berkeley Mall, Downtown Goldsboro. We bought shirts of any sleeve length, shorts, pants, jackets, hats, mittens, shoes, boots, sandals, and more. To avoid suspicion, I wrote a check that I stole from the bank and placed it under the Nova Vegan government's account. The total cost of all of the clothes and shoes was around $14,000,000. One of the clerks was suspicious, knowing the government had never done that before. Just when Cali and I were about to leave the store, two officers from the secret police saw us.

"Hey!" one of them shouted.

We made a run for it. Apparently, the clerk labeled Cali and me shoplifters after realizing that I paid him with a stolen check, alerting the officers. They took their guns from their holsters. My guess was that the clerk was a Telepath. That was bad. The officers were shooting at us, and the civilians ducked behind benches and jumped inside the stores to avoid the flying bullets. Fear poured through our bodies and minds as Cali and I turned toward the exit right in front of us. But we chose not to go through the exit. We held hands, thought of the warehouse, and teleported, but not before we heard one last gunshot.

The good news was that we made it back alive. The bad news was unpleasant. One of the lower-class teenagers, a Telepath, noticed something on my "left shoulder," as she said. I looked and saw there was a bullet hole. I'd been shot. Blood was draining out of me. Dropping the bags of clothes and shoes, and looking at Cali in fear, I fell over. Worried, she caught me in time and brought me over to her room. Blood was dripping on the floor, and I was losing consciousness, my eyes slowly closing. Everything became a blur before going dark.

I thought I was going to die, but then, I woke up. Was I in Heaven, or in my Dream World? Cali told me that I was out for three hours. She pointed at my shoulder, and to my surprise, the bullet wound was gone. It was on the day that I learned she also possessed more than one power. She was a Teleporter, Healer, Telekinesist, Element Manipulator, and a Returner. Before she healed me, she used telekinesis to extract the bullet from my shoulder. Had it remained there, it would've dissolved, and lead poisoning would have killed me, unless blood loss killed me first.

Then, an idea struck me. "Cali, how long does it take to revive the dead?"

"Around thirty minutes," she answered. "Why?"

"Because I know someone who died two years back. And if it's possible, if these people have relatives that died, can you do that for them, too?"

It was on that day when Cali told me that she hadn't run away from her family. She ran away from a foster home. Her parents were arrested and killed for possessing more than one power, while she was forced to live with the other orphans. She doesn't know where they were, and therefore, she could not find them. And if she could not find them, she would not revive them from the dead. The lower-class children, the orphans, had parents that were mutilated, crushed, blasted to oblivion, and/or burned into ashes. Feeling sad for them, all I could do was show empathy for Cali. From that moment on, I learned the four requirements of what needed to be done before making the decision of resurrecting the dead. That stayed with me.

***

At Evergreen Memorial Cemetery in Princeton, Cali and I teleported to my mother's grave, the one with the bouquet of flowers carved on top. It read:

In Loving Memory of Fedora Melody Weston-Bernard
She was a beloved wife, a loving mother, a beautiful sister, a precious aunt, and a wonderful friend to the end.
August 15, 2113 – September 16, 2151

I feared that we would get caught by surveillance and end up being sued for digging a family member's grave, but it was the only way we could recover her corpse. Determination came to me, and I was excited at the fact that my mother was going to come back to life. Inside at the bottom of the grave, the coffin was still there. Digging edges around the coffin was very important, preventing dirt from getting inside once we opened it. We wouldn't want to get dirt all over Mom before reviving her.

It was time; time for Mom to come back to the World of the Living. But when we opened the marble coffin, her body was not there. It was gone, just like Cali's parents when they were taken away for execution. I didn't want to believe it. It had to be a dream, but my mother always told me to confront reality rather than escape from it. She wouldn't want me in denial. I was stronger than that. Instead, I got out from the grave, frightened and sad before sitting in my fetal position crying after seeing the empty coffin.

The Nova Vegan government must've found the last of the Returners and killed them to make sure those without resurrection powers, including Mom, stayed dead. They took the bodies from the graves to make certain the resurrection process would never happen. Those bodies with resurrections end up cremated. Cali, with tears rolling from her eyes, sat next to me after coming out from the grave, placing her hands on my shoulders. We failed. My mother's body was gone. We didn't know how, when, or why it happened. Nor was there any point in finding the body after what transpired in the cemetery. I'm sorry, Mom. I thought I found a way to bring you back, but not anymore. I was to live with that sadness and disappointment for the rest of my life, even though I had no choice but to move on and live.

XIX- Phoebe Truman

Present- I'm glad that Ferenc returned from the Afterlife. I don't know what I would've done if he hadn't come back. Probably be in Kent's shoes and steal to survive. I don't know much about his sister and cousin, but I know that he can handle himself. His life in the streets was proof of that. I was also surprised that Cali had so much potential in her, especially on how she was able to bring my older brother back to life.

While I was waiting for Kent, Gabriella and Riley to return with their stuff and relaxing on the ceiling rails of the abandon warehouse, Ferenc was on the lookout for the secret police at the entrance. So far, there was no sign of them. At least Kent managed to get the officers pursuing us off our backs. We would've wound up like Principal White. I remembered the Captain of the Secret Police mentioning, *"Until we caught him and finished what we started!"* That left me wondering. Then again, Cali was involved with Kent. Did Cali know about it? That was what I was planning to ask her after I landed on the ground safely and retracted my wings.

***

In the large bathroom, what used to be the loading dock, Cali manipulated water from the sprinklers that she stole. She placed it inside the water tank hidden underneath the floor. I was curious about why she did that and why she didn't connect the sinks, toilets, and showers to the water pipes. I had a feeling that the answer was about to be explained. I said, "I guess you already know what happened to the lower-class citizens."

"Yes, I know," she said, closing the floor door, with a sad look on her face. "Four days after Kent left, the lower-class citizens and their families left, ready to start a new life in Nova Vega. Yesterday, I stole one of the newspapers and learned that the secret police captured them and cast them out into the wastelands after the lower-class citizens spent years hiding from them. They all tried to get back in, trying to prove they can fit in, but after the secret police turned deaf ears on them all, some of them were shot and killed. The rest of them fled in fear and never returned. After that, just when I was about to take a shower to wash my worries away, I noticed that the water didn't work."

I responded, "That would explain the school water fountains not running."

"The government cut off the water supplies, under the assumption that it would 'wash away the problem,' the secret police said. In reality, they did that to punish the country for helping the poor and the homeless. It's their way of saying either to stop helping the needy, or die of thirst and dehydration."

I felt my jaw stiffen with anger. Hunting down Pasdúnami was one thing, and forcing Kent back to his father's home against his will was another thing, but cutting off water supplies? I couldn't believe the government would go that far. All the lower-class citizens wanted was to get their lives back and fit in with society, and the government took it away from them. So much for sharing is caring. Even if our enemy did believe in that moral, they would abuse it for personal gain, as Cali said, "They pushed survival of the fittest too far. Another way of saying salvation for themselves, damnation for the rest."

Relaxing my jaw, I looked at Cali in curiosity and asked, "Speaking of, when did you become a Pasdúnamis anyway?"

Her sadness faded as she answered, "I was born one alongside my parents. Apart from the Flyer, Element Manipulator, Healer, Animator, and Morpher Tribes, the Teleporter Tribe was the ally of the Pasdúnamis Tribe."

"My family and I were born Pasdúnami, too," I said.

Her eyes widened in wonder, and she asked, "Really?"

"Yeah. Despite that, my parents are the leaders of the Flyer Tribe."

"And my parents were the leaders of the Teleporter Tribe."

My eyes widened in disbelief. The leaders of the Teleporter Tribe? I wondered what happened to them. When I asked her, we both sat down on the floor and she began speaking, "Since I already told Kent about my life before coming here, I might as well tell you, too. It was on the night before the forgotten Martin Luther King, Jr. Day over three years ago. My parents were political activists, supporting the rights of the lower-class citizens and seeking to end the banishment in hope of giving all of Nova Vega a future. They were going to have the petition made public on the very same day. But one night, the government caught my parents on surveillance, using more than one power; teleportation, element manipulation, and heal, exposing themselves as Pasdúnami."

My eyes widened in dismay, and I asked, "Did the secret police know about your status, too?"

"Of course not. They didn't see me using more than one power on surveillance. They would've succeeded in finding out, too, if my parents hadn't told me to leave and run for my life. I didn't look back. I teleported to North Carolina MENTOR, the secret orphanage. I stole my first newspaper the next day and learned that my parents were executed via firing squad." Her eyes filled with tears and I felt my heart break. "I cried for hours, knowing that I was all alone. All I had left was a photo of Mom and Dad," she said pounding her right fist on the floor hard. "But it was taken away from me and torn to shreds the next month! Those cruel and insensitive bullies provoked my anger and I beat the crud out of them! I was going to give them their just desserts, but I ended up getting into trouble. My punishment, unfair as it was; I was sent to my room with no meals for a week. I ran away the same night and came to this warehouse, my home away from Hell."

Showing pity, I felt sorry for what she had gone through, and I asked her, "How old were you when your parents died?"

"I was ten years old when they died, two months before my eleventh birthday, and I'd been alone for seven months since running away from the orphanage; until I met Kent three years ago."

"I felt just the same when my parents went away last year," I said.

Her eyes showed curiosity and she asked, "What happened to them?"

"They went on a business trip, but they never came back. Ferenc and I didn't get a single letter, no phone calls, nor notes, or text messages— not even a single voice message from either of them. Every day, in secret, I had always feared that something bad happened to them, something I haven't told anyone, until now," I knitted my eyebrows, feeling both sadness and fear. "I worry that they ended up sharing your parents' fates. Either that, or they don't care about us anymore. The irony is that I waited for them to return, but I didn't know when. I worry about them every day since they departed and left Ferenc in charge. All they ever left us was a checkbook. He knew how to use it, and whenever I needed money for meals, he would help me out. But when my brother was busy, my friends would help me out."

I continued with a smile, "I'm a better cook, and my brother is a better cleaner. But on rare occasions, we would switch around." My smile faded back to a sad frown. "Other than my concern for my parents' safety, I started to worry about Seifer, Mark, Valeda, and Asteria, especially after what happened today back at the school. I know I worry too much, but I can't help it when it comes to my friends and family in situations like that."

"Don't worry so much about people, Pheebs," she said, as we stood back up and walked out of the bathroom into the massive main hall, smiling as she put her arm around my shoulders. "As my parents once said, *Don't worry about the dead. Only worry about the living and those who are incapable of love, kindness, and compassion.*"

My right eyebrow raised in confusion at first, until she continued. "In some situations, there's a time to help people and a time, not to give up, but to know when to wait for the right moment."

"Then, why didn't you bring your parents back to life?"

We stopped walking and she released me, walking three steps away from me.

"Oh!" I said lowering my head in shame. "Forgive me, Cali. I didn't..."

"No, Phoebe," she responded, shaking her head, causing me to lift my head and looking at her as my shame faded. "Quite the opposite. Actually, I'm glad you asked. You see, it's because after my parents were executed, their bodies were dumped at the wasteland, where all of the dead go when they're executed. People go out, none come back in. Even if that were possible to come back in without getting caught by the Watchers, the walls are under surveillance, too, and they contain pressure sensors, making it impossible to avoid traps and the secret police."

I face-palmed and responded, "Good point." I looked back at her and said, "That explains the Flyers that defied the government, trying to escape but ending up shot down by missiles."

Before we had a chance to go to her room to talk more, Kent, Gabriella, and Riley returned via teleportation, startling us and catching our attention. That was fast, I thought. And to our surprise, Riley walked slumped as he carried a black folder filled with files. Why would he bring it along with their stuff? Was it full of school stuff, or classified information that we weren't aware of?

"We need to talk back at Cali's room," said Kent, his expression serious.

"It's worse than we thought," said Riley, agitated.

"What's this about?" Cali asked in a concerned tone.

"Let's go to your room first, and we'll explain everything."

XX- Phoebe Truman

Five years earlier- The day after my birthday, we moved to 104 E Peter Street in Goldsboro. It was hard for Ferenc to say goodbye to his friends, but my parents always say that when departing from a place where your friends still live, it's not goodbye, as in forever. It is farewell, which was usually difficult for my brother to comprehend since we weren't going to see Mom and Dad for a long while.

After we moved, Ferenc developed abandonment issues. It's been that way since we moved to North Carolina. To him, life was never the same without his old friends. He was afraid that with them out of his life, they would forget about him. Not everyone forgets their friends, but like I said, he had abandonment issues. It even continued when I made friends with Seifer, Mark, Valeda, and Asteria, causing him to experience jealousy and bitter selfishness. We had our quarrels from time to time over the situation. And at the same time, I made enemies with Sirena Peyton. And every time she picked on me, four of my friends always backed me up.

***

Three years later, I accidentally used more than one power in front of them. I wanted to run away from them that day, but Seifer stopped me. I was under the belief that he was going to turn me over to the secret police, until he told me that having more than one power was cool. I felt relieved that day, and it was the first time someone had ever acknowledged and accepted me for who I am. Having more than one power didn't matter to him. And it didn't matter to Mark, Valeda, and Asteria either.

***

They swore to keep it a secret, and it took around nine months before they won Ferenc's trust. His was not as easy to achieve as it was with Mom and Dad's trust. He feared they would betray and turn me over to the secret police. Even my brother Ferenc kept his status as a Pasdúnamis a secret from his old friends, never regretting that secrecy. How would he know? He didn't show more than one power to them either. For all we knew, they could've been open-minded with the idea from the start. But to Ferenc, it was best not to take any chances,

93

viewing everyone around him as unpredictable. What would be the point of having friends if one doesn't experience taking risks? Then again, my brother would have a point. There's a time for truth, and a time, not for lies, but for silence.

And that night, my brother warmed up to Seifer, Mark, Valeda, and Asteria upon realizing that they could be trusted, and he accepted them into his life, whether it was out of reluctance, or through a change of heart. In celebration of letting them into his heart, Ferenc snuck the six of us into the Forbidden Zone to watch some movies at the ruins of the UEC Theater in Goldsboro. The ticket booth, arcade games, and the concession stand were busted, but at least we managed to bring our own snacks and some movies. Mark, being a creative idealist, brought his own projector since all of the movie projectors in theaters were nothing but scrap metal. Valeda, who was known to camp with her family every summer and believed in being prepared, brought some popcorn, nachos, and soda. Asteria, who enjoyed the night sky every night before bedtime, movie time, and any time, brought some candy, blankets, and pillows. The movies I brought with me were *Blade Runner, Divergent, V for Vendetta, Elysium, The Fifth Element, The Lego Movie,* and *Planet of the Apes Original Film Series.*

Watching dystopian movies were forbidden in Nova Vega, but my family and I always hid them well to keep the Nova Vegan government from confiscating them. Besides, the movie theater that we snuck into hadn't been used for over a century. The movie stage was a bit ruined, but there were plenty of seats for the six of us. Thankfully, Seifer had teleportation, and he'd been Mark's technological partner for years.

Since Ferenc was already eighteen years old, he supervised us when the first movie we watched was *V for Vendetta,* as it was one of the three R-rated movies. Too bad we never had a Shadow Gallery of our own, like V did. The part about the lesbian actress's backstory always made me cry from beginning to end. Valeda cried the hardest, and Asteria held her tight to comfort her. Mark, much to mine and Seifer's amusement, burst out laughing. As much as my brother's worry about not wanting any of us to get caught, he loved the comedy sketch scene with the main antagonist breaking his glass of milk in rage. He was right. That was funny, even for Asteria.

Seifer picked *Blade Runner,* another R-rated dystopian movie. I could see why his pet dove was named after the main villain. Whenever Ferenc and I watched that movie, we always argued about whether or not the protagonist Deckard was a replicant. He believed so. I didn't. In fact, that debate existed for almost two centuries.

Just when we were about to watch *Elysium,* which was Valeda's choice, one of the secret police officers spotted us, startling us at the last minute. Seifer and Mark, who managed to make an army of mannequins out of remaining red chairs, unplugged the projector while the rest of us ran out of the stage through the emergency exit. Two of our friends met up with us, and we teleported back to the Truman Residence. From there, we had our slumber party and continued watching dystopian movies until we fell asleep. I couldn't believe that even the secret police would search the Forbidden Zone for Pasdúnami, yet spotted us. They scared the shit out of me. They must've been looking for me the whole time after the incident back at Pittsburgh. Why else would they have spotted me, my brother, and my friends that night? It didn't matter. On the positive side, no one at my new school knew about me thanks to Ferenc, otherwise, I would've been done for.

***

The following mid-morning, Mom found out what we did the previous night due to having telepathy. She was not happy with me and Ferenc for what we did, but Seifer, Mark, Valeda, and Asteria were lucky. They were told that it was a good thing that Mom and Dad would not tell their families that they were with us at the Forbidden Zone. Seifer's parents would be worried, Mark's mother would disown him, which would have him cast out of Nova Vega, Valeda would be sent to live with her grandmother in Georgia, and Asteria would be homeschooled for the rest of her life. Three out of four, talk about harsh punishment. And who could blame Seifer's parents for worrying about for his safety? Better to keep things in the dark than suffer the harshest of consequences.

***

In the living room, Mom and Dad told Ferenc and me that they were going to be on a business trip for a year, and my brother was placed in charge of the house until their return. A year seemed like a very long time. From that moment on, I worried for my parents a lot more than I did for anyone else. And whenever I worry, Ferenc would sing "God's Raven" to me. He only knew twelve lines, but I didn't mind at all. It was the only time he found out my worry for our parents, but I kept it to myself for the rest of the time.

XXI- Kent Bernard

Present- The cat was out of the bag. Well, for Gabriella in front of Dad anyway. But not me. Not unless I revealed myself as a Pasdúnamis. Riley would do the same if he wasn't so afraid of my father. Yet there we were, face to face with him. My sister aimed her bow and arrow at him after materializing it from running tap water. I was still confused as to how the water worked in our house and not at the school. That was something we would never know.

"So, you committed heresy now, Gabriella?!" Dad rebuked.

"Pasdúnami were never heretics, Dad!" she scolded. "They were labeled as such because the government feared losing power and authority, the two things they deemed more precious to them than the lives of Nova Vega! It suited the political officials of this system ill! Don't you remember the old saying made by Lord Acton?! *Power tends to corrupt, and absolute power corrupts absolutely!*"

"That old fool was afraid of power he didn't understand!"

"Because the government wanted you to believe that! They rule Nova Vega through fear! Trust, freedom, and love are meaningless to them! You know it's true! Even Mom knew that! In fact, she always knew what they were capable of, and you agreed with her!" She lowered her bow and arrow, her anger turning to sadness. "What happened to that same father we once knew?!"

He pointed upward with his right index finger and responded in bitterness, "That man died alongside his wife a long time ago!"

Wait a minute! Something was not right. And for the first time, I was about to read Dad's mind, but instead there was a sight, a terrifying image I had never seen before. It wasn't the same dream I had two nights before. It was a different dream. But wait. This was new. It was like I'd developed a whole new power- Memory Reading.

***

And I was right. I remembered that part. It was the day Mom collapsed on the floor. Gabriella and I left for school before that happened. Mom drank coffee with milk on the way back from the grocery store. Then, I saw my father the night before my mother collapsed from the incurable illness. He took a canteen of coffee out from the refrigerator, opened it up on the counter, and poured a strange substance from the vial. The substance was green and when poured, the color vanished, blended in with the coffee.

Returning after she drank the coffee in the car and coming inside the house, Mom brought in a first round of groceries, but collapsed on the living room floor, and the food and meal essentials fell from the bags. Hold on. The incurable illness. Mom collapsing on the floor after taking a sip of her coffee on the way home. Dad pouring a strange substance inside the coffee, and the same coffee she drank. No!

***

I snapped out of it and looked at Dad in horror. Lowering my eyebrows together in the mixture of outrage and fury, I screamed. I pinned him to the dining room wall with telekinesis, much to his eye-widening shock as he looked directly at me. I said, "Now, it all makes sense. It was *you*! Mom didn't have an incurable illness! You killed her!"

Jaws dropping, Gabriella and Riley looked at me in shock and back at Dad in disbelief. She asked in tears, "Is this true?! You killed Mom?!"

"And don't bother lying either!" I said in bitterness. "I can read minds as well."

He lowered his eyes before responding, "Hmph! Looks like there's no point in hiding it now! Yes, I killed your mother! She was a Pasdúnamis, too!"

"What was that substance you poured into her coffee?!"

"A new type of poison," he grinned deviously. "Solaride, the answer to Nova Vega's Pasdúnami problem. It coats bullets, knives, and consumable substances, making a Pasdúnamis very, very sick and in six days, they're dead."

I threw my father to the wall hard. I teleported in front of him, grabbed him by the collar of his shirt, and punched him in the face, much to Riley's shock. Blinded by rage, screaming with tears sliding down my face, I punched Dad so much that he was getting bruises on the right side of his forehead and cheek. He even had a nosebleed, and my right fist was coated in his blood. Gabriella couldn't sit by and watch me beat our father into a bloody pulp. She grabbed my right arm and reprimanded, "Stop it, Kent! If you keep this up, he'll die, and you'll end up no better than him!"

"He killed our mother!" I yelled.

"And perhaps many other Pasdúnami before and after her! Didn't you ever think about that?!"

"She's right, man!" said Riley, walking toward both of us with concern on his face. "Uncle Jacob can wait another time! Right now, our top priority is leaving Nova Vega!"

"NO!!!" Dad yelled.

He punched me to the ground, forcing me off of him. He looked at all three of us and shouted, "No one is going anywhere!" Dad pointed out the window. "You

97

all think it's safe outside the walls! All there is out there are rubble, ruins, and death!"

"How can you be sure?!" Riley yelled. "You've never even been outside of it, and neither has the rest of Nova Vega!"

"I don't have to be out there! The government is always right about the outside world, and if you three won't accept it, then you are no relatives of mine and are now traitors of the country!"

"We're not traitors to the country or the people!" said Gabriella, as she aimed her bow and arrow at him again. "We're only traitors to the people running it, and it takes one to view one as such!"

Looking up at the ceiling, she aimed at the chandelier, shot it, causing sparks from the light bulb, conjuring up fire. Once she morphed the bow and arrows into a floating water sphere, my sister fused water from her hand with fire to create a massive smokescreen, giving the three of us a chance to escape from the Bernard Residence. There was no way we would come back here. But our path from the front porch was blocked by none other than Hestia.

"Where do you three think you're going?" she asked in a stern tone.

"We're going to my house," Riley answered. "We..."

"Hold on."

She looked at us directly in the eyes. That's a Telepath's way of using their power when beginning to read minds. Her eyes widened in realization and disbelief and said, "I understand," she looked at me and Gabriella. "And don't worry. I'll take good care of Rosy for you."

Hestia took out a notepad and pencil, wrote something down and tore the page out, giving it to Riley.

"Teleport your animals, including your newts, to *this* address, and leave Jacob with me. Now, go. Get as far away from here as you three can."

"Will we see you again?" Gabriella asked.

"That is up to fate," Hestia looked at me. "And Kent, I know you'll never see me as any more than a symbol of your father's selfishness, and you have every right to be angry at me after what you've been through. But you need to think about this— who is the true enemy?"

I was skeptical to believe her, and after finding out what Dad did to Mom, I would like to believe that she was on the government's side as well. But seeing her give the address to Riley about where to put the animals for protection, and help train Gabriella in secret during my absence, I wasn't sure what to believe anymore. I even swore to myself that my truce with her was only temporary, and after that, I never wanted to see her again.

Surprisingly, and much to my confusion, she gave the three of us a hug, and my sister and cousin hugged her back. Oddly enough, I reluctantly hugged her back, only as a sign of thanking her for the help and nothing more. After that, she went inside the house. The address on the paper said- 400 Roth Ave. Philadelphia, PA. But there was no such address, but if Hestia said to have my cousin's animals sent to that address, we would need to trust her judgment. My sister was glad that I gave Hestia a chance, even if it was for once. Riley, as Gabriella and I held on to his hand, teleported the three of us to the Weston Residence- 817 Dashner Blvd.

***

In front of us was a blue house with two floors and an attic. In the backyard, there was a fountain of newts that were the same color and breed as Newt. There was a domestic pig that my cousin called Chuck. At our left was an Alaskan Malamute named Winston. The cage had a black jaguar Riley named Alby. Wow! My cousin really was into *The Maze Runner*. I wonder what happened to Teresa, Jeff, and Ben.

Okay, Phoebe and I may have told you the truth about books in Nova Vega, but we never told you all of it. In fact, the Nova Vegan government kept some books, but the ones that had fantasy and dystopian genres in them were banned around the same time fiction writing was banned. Since then, most of the books with those genres were sold in hidden black markets; those that weren't under surveillance. Same way with movies, video games, and other types of media. People bought them and kept them hidden. And whenever we got pets of our own, we formed a tradition of naming animals after deceased fictional characters in the dystopian genre, like Phoebe, Riley, and I did. So many pets named after dead fictional dystopian characters, yet most of us preferred to name them after heroes.

Anyway, Riley had to say farewell to his pets and Newt before teleporting them to the address Hestia wrote down. He thought of it, and they vanished upon him touching each and every one of them. Again, he had to wash his hands after touching the newts. Thankfully, they were the last animals he touched.

***

Riley packed as much stuff as possible from clothes and bed supplies to camping supplies, food to drinks to school books and cameras. Gabriella was annoyed when he had packed so much. Sure, he didn't have to bring a lot of stuff, but Nova Vega was already enemy territory for us anyway. Thankfully, my sister and I managed to teleport the stuff we packed before we got interrupted. The food and drinks, we never got a chance to bring, and we were glad that our cousin managed that.

Riley was done, but he spotted something at his right upon walking into the hallway. My sister was right to be annoyed, feeling that we got enough stuff to bring as it was, needing enough room for Phoebe and Ferenc's stuff also. With a stunned look on his face, our cousin Riley got out of the bedroom at the end of the hallway with his stuff teleported back to the abandoned warehouse. In his right hand was a black folder with a lot of files inside, which was found hidden inside a wooden wardrobe.

Irritated, Gabriella said, "Riley, this is not the time to be bringing homework."

"It's not homework," he answered. "Look!"

He showed us the front of the folder with the title that said, "Pasdúnami." He opened it and showed us the form with a signature- R. E. Weston, Captain of the Nova Vegan Secret Police. And there was a fingerprint imprinted next to the signature in blood— R. E. Weston. To mine and my sister's shock, we saw another name under the list of secret police officers; J. A. Bernard. It all made sense. Our father was part of the secret police, and being a lawyer was a daytime job. And the person he was working for was none other than Rex Eaton Weston, Riley's abusive father. Why would Rex have Dad murder Mom? She was his sister, so he had his brother-in-law kill her. Why? With no time to waste, no time to answer these questions, and not wanting to stick around for Uncle Rex's return, we needed to get back to the warehouse and fast, and the three of us teleported back there along with the rest of our stuff.

***

Phoebe and Cali were confused at first when we returned, but Riley showed them the folder that he stole from his father's bedroom. We met up in Cali's room to discuss everything. Looking through the files, we saw that it contained pictures of the Pasdúnami who were already killed with X's marked in their own blood. Her parents were in those files, too. Her father had brown hair and green eyes, while her mother had red hair and blue eyes, making Cali's hair and eye colors genetically mixed together as one. According to one of the files, her father's name was Joshua, and he belonged in three Tribes: Teleporter, Healer, and Element Manipulator. Cali's mother's name was Sarah, and she belonged in three Tribes as well: Teleporter, Telekinesist, and Returner. They looked like very nice people, and from what she told me long ago.

Anyway, the next file was about Mom. She belonged in six Tribes: Hypnotist, Teleporter, Telepath, Element Manipulator, Returner, and Healer. Three Returners, yet one of them still lived. I was still pissed off at my father for ending my mother's life, even if it was under Uncle Rex's orders. Perhaps he needed the money from his sister to fund the production of Solaride, to exterminate every Pasdúnami spotted throughout Nova Vega. I read Cali's mind, who wondered if my mother met her parents before. I wondered the same thing.

Going through the files, some of them were not marked, including the ones of Phoebe and Ferenc's parents. That must've meant that they were still alive. Her worries were over as she sighed in relief. Even her brother was glad that she could finally relax, as if he knew about her, afraid for their lives from the start. But that didn't mean they were completely safe, and Phoebe was right to worry about their parents. As long as they were Pasdúnami, they were still the prey,

100

nd they could be in big trouble. Before we had a chance to look through more of he files, we jumped in fright, startled by the sound of sirens coming from outside he warehouse.

Ferenc was the first to look through the window, and his eyes widened in hock. He looked at us and exclaimed, "It's the secret police! They found us! And ve're surrounded!"

XXII- Kent Bernard

Six days earlier- I still felt bad not being able to recover my mother's corpse in time. Then again, I never realized that the Returners, if there were still more in Nova Vega, still existed until it was too late. Whatever happened to it, there was no telling where it was now. On the bright side, at least I knew that everything was going to be alright. Mom would want me to move on anyway, because bothering to look for the body would take too long and increase the chances of getting caught, which would be days later. If her body was still in the grave, she wouldn't mind being resurrected. Even the Maker wouldn't mind, because He knew she didn't deserve to die. And that was long before I found out that Dad killed her through Rex's orders.

The dreams I had were always the same after I ran away from home. There were injections, death, and a man dressed like a priest hovering over a girl on the operating table. I usually woke up screaming during those times. And when I did, Cali would cover my mouth and tell me that they were only dreams. It didn't matter. It plagued me from that day on. But at least they never distracted me from stealing stuff that were shipped and produced by the Nova Vegan government. I developed two more powers during those days— telepathy and element manipulation. They were not easy to master alongside teleportation, and it took hours to weeks to control them.

For telepathy, I had a headache for an entire week after reading a lot of minds near or far. I was an accident prone at first with element manipulation; hence accidentally causing Cali's hair to get puffed up from the electricity, and the warehouse nearly flooded from all of the water during one of my showers. It took a while, but I managed to get better control over them as the weeks were flowing by.

And three days before I was arrested, it was time for me to be on my own. I was already a twelfth grader. It was time for me to homeschool myself. After learning the methods of self-teaching for educational purposes and gaining better focus and application, there was no need for me to have a teacher anymore. But self-teaching with college materials was about to be tough. Still, I knew that

I would manage it. Cali had the same faith in me. After all, if I couldn't become a fiction writer in public, then I would have to become one in secret; use a secret alias since I didn't want to risk getting exposed and caught.

There was no one left in the abandoned warehouse. Once I departed, it was only going to be Cali, continuing to survive on her own, and provide community service in secret. It wouldn't be the same without me around. Look at me; seventeen years old for eighteen days, been away from home for three years, and I was about to miss the warehouse, which was also my home away from Hell. It was time for me to find myself a new home away from Hell.

Packing up food, water, clothes, and twelfth grade textbooks, Cali came into my old room.

"Are you sure you're going to be alright, Kent?" she asked.

"Yes, Cali. I'm sure," I said, after zipping up my bag.

"You know, you're more than welcome to visit anytime. After all, you and I are partners in crime for life."

"If I find a way back inside Nova Vega, I'll be sure to do that."

Her eyes widened in surprise. She told me that going outside of Nova Vega was very dangerous. It was also the place where her parents' bodies were dumped after they were executed. But I assured her that there was a possibility that civilization existed outside the walls, whether the government wanted us to believe so or not. There was always some way to get back inside the walls. Inside, I might be afraid at first, but without fear, there was no bravery; for one cannot exist without the other. If I could survive the streets of Nova Vega, then I was also determined to survive outside no matter how difficult. And someday, I would return and help restore the world through Nova Vega's help, even if the government and its followers refuse.

"No matter what they say, we can't be ignorant about the outside world forever," I continued, as I pointed at the door before looking back at her. "If we don't find out what's out there, then we may as well be the only civilization left, and the rest of the world would really be a barren wasteland forever. But until then, I'm going to spend the rest of my educational life in Nova Vega."

She was doubtful at first, but she relaxed, feeling confident that I might be right about outside the walls. She said to me, as we walked to the front of the warehouse, "Be careful out there, Kent. And I wish you the best of luck."

"Thank you."

We stopped near the door, and for the first time, we looked deep into each other's eyes. My heart was racing, my eyes filled with happiness, and for the first time in our lives, we fell deeply in love with one another. Before I departed from the abandoned warehouse, we kissed passionately as if it was to be our last. Walking forward, I waved farewell to Cali, and she did the same. That was the last time we ever saw each other until six days later. Three days after my departure, I got busted by Morpher Police Officers at the condemned college in the Forbidden Zone and sent back to my home the next day. And that led back to where my story began; getting surrounded by the secret police at the same place I ran away to and back again.

XXIII- Phoebe Truman

Present- Surrounded by the secret police?! How did they find us?! It wasn't even under surveillance! Even Kent and the others were dumbfounded. Not Cali, because she mentioned earlier that her traps would take care of them. Then again, the secret police surrounded the place. There was a slight chance that they would avoid her traps. And when they entered the front door, I was correct. The captain, or should I say Rex, used his telekinesis to stop the tranquilizer darts in their tracks. He reached out for the catapults with his right hand and grasped tight, crushing them into messy woodchips and bended metal spikes. Noticing the falling cages, Rex aimed his left palm and stopped them in their tracks. Grasping them tight, he bent them into metallic balls before dropping them and the ruined catapults before lowering his arms.

Cali was not pleased with what he did. Rex had his officers surround the six of us as we walked into the massive room. And teleporting in front of us, much to our jaw-dropping disbelief, were Sirena, Cass, and Calvin. They still had guns with them.

"Get out of my home, you bastards!" Cali screamed, as she manipulated part of the metal floor and materialized it into a gun.

"Silence!" yelled Rex, who used telekinesis to freeze her with his mind. "You've been in hiding from the government for far too long, Daughter of Joshua and Sarah Ross!"

"Leave her alone, Dad!" Riley scolded, as he stood in the way.

"So, you found out the truth, Riley. Just like your mother, always nosy and rebellious."

"And for the right reason, too. Now, remove the mask. It's already damaged from our last encounter. Don't make us damage it further."

"Mind your manners!"

"Or what, Captain Weston?! You going to kill me?! You already gave me a death threat before when you abused me! Then again, you planned to kill me anyway!"

Hesitant at first, Rex unfroze Cali and removed his mask, revealing his pale skin, greying-blonde hair, hazel eyes, and a full beard. He was truly becoming an old man, almost at his mid-40s. First, he was a child abuser and a cruel ex-husband. Now, he was a hypocritical, murdering, remorseless monster. Not only that, but he was also a traitor to the Pasdúnami and his family. For whatever reason he had, having his sister killed, I could tell it was not a good sign.

"If it's any consolation, Riley, I was never going to let you live after I wipe out all of the Pasdúnami," said Rex.

"Then, why betray your family?" he asked bitterly.

Angry, and with his right fist clutching, Rex pointed at his son with his right index finger and responded, "That's none of your concern."

"It is my concern. I'm your son. Remember?"

"I saw you as a slave rather than family. In fact," he spread his arms wide with a cruel smile on his face, "my real family is the government."

"Then, you're a monster!" I shouted, catching his enraged attention as I took out a rock that I'd picked up back at the school grounds.

I materialized it into a gun and shot at him. But he reached out his right arm and used telekinesis to stop the bullet and grab it. That was a cheap shot. Then again, who said he was a fair player? He was one of the bad guys after all. He even gave me a cruel smile, which I found disturbing, and said, "Surely, you could do better than that, Daughter of Adam and Mary. Oh, that's right. It's not going to happen for you."

He nodded at Sirena, who aimed her gun at me, while giving me a cruel grin. I closed my eyes, but Rex used his telekinesis to force my eyes open and lower my arm. Obsessed and stubborn, he wanted me to look at Sirena, expecting me to look at the last person I would ever see before I die.

And just when she pulled the trigger, the bullet stopped near my forehead and went through the helix of Cass's right ear, causing him to cover it up and scream in pain as it squirted blood. And thanks to my Telekinesist genetics, I cancelled Rex's powers and looked to who stopped the bullet from penetrating my brain, literally. Much to my astonishment, it was Kent, whose eyes, filled with fierce rage, looked directly at Cass, while Cass screamed in pain.

Calvin lowered his gun and attempted to help his brother out. Ferenc used his telekinesis to shoot the tranquilizer darts that were still levitated at the officers that surrounded us. It was just Rex, Sirena, and the Emmerich Brothers. With our enemy distracted by Cass's agony, my brother gained the upper hand by teleporting behind Calvin and gave an atomic wedgie, making two brothers in a row that got wedgified. Sirena was raving mad at what he did after Calvin blindly ran into her. She was going to shoot at Ferenc, but unexpectedly, her hair was on fire. Cali managed to manipulate the heat inside the building and mix it with our enemy's hair, making it combust and burst into flames. Sirena noticed and screamed in fear, running to different places to look for water, or anything to douse her burning hair. Two idiots with a bitch beaten by six outlaws of Nova Vega, that's funny, yet intense.

"ENOUGH!!!" Rex yelled in fury, as he undid the wedgie, the bleeding, and the burning with his powers, looking directly at us. "Big mistake to mess with us, you selfish brats!"

"They deserved it," Kent said with a sarcastic smirk.

"And *you* deserve only death, just like Fedora!"

Uh-oh! Not a good idea to provoke the captain of the secret police! Kent was stunned from what he heard, causing his smirk to fade into eye-widening disbelief. His cruel uncle made a wicked grin and said, "Yes, *I* was the one who had my sister executed. But she wasn't the only Pasdúnamis, and neither am I, nor my dead wife."

Riley was devastated from what he heard, jaws dropping in horrifying disbelief. Dead? Then, that meant that the part about his parents having a divorce was a lie. He didn't want to believe it, but he took out the folder he stole and attempt to look for the photo. Rex, however, used telekinesis to take it away and took out the file with the photo of his ex-wife, marked X in blood. She had black hair, green eyes, and tan skin. It all became clear to Riley. Fedora was not his father's first victim. His ex-wife, whose name was Tess Weston, was his first victim.

As Rex walked around the six of us like a tiger circling his prey, waiting for the right moment to strike, he told us his reason for joining the Nova Vegan government, murdering Tess and Fedora, and becoming Captain of the Nova Vegan Secret Police. Sirena was still not pleased with his hypocrisy after all this time, but instead of convincing him not to say anymore, she reluctantly listened, as she already learned that he was related to Kent, Gabriella, and Riley. It was to be the last time, as a family, that he would ever share with them a story of his life. The Emmerich Brothers were interested in hearing what he had to say, eager and possibly determined to take the story to their future advantages.

In truth, the Pasdúnami were underground rebels, seeking to end the tyranny of the government itself. Fedora and Jacob, whom the latter was also a Pasdúnamis, were selected as the leaders of the rebel cell. Rex, on the other hand, was only the co-leader alongside Tess. Their mission was to deliver a certain disc to the central broadcast network, revealing the truth about the Nova Vegan government and its plans for its citizens. Fedora and Jacob believed that it would give freedom back to the people of Nova Vega. Rex's agenda for liberation was the same, but his was different from their agenda. He wanted to develop a new government. While Fedora wanted to unite the country with the United States and the world, her brother wanted to keep Nova Vega isolated, under the impression that it was the only inhabitable and suitable place left.

Fedora never saw Rex again after that, but Tess remained hers and Jacob's contact, until her husband killed her right in front of the government, who went to their home to have them arrested, tried, and executed. He betrayed the Pasdúnami and joined the Nova Vegan government. With Chancellor Jelen's permission, Rex formed the Nova Vegan Secret Police, making him both its captain and its leader. Their loyalty was to her and to her alone. With their loyalty to her unquestioned, they made certain that laws remained enforced making them superiors to law enforcement. Some of her men joined the organization. The rest of the members were sleeper agents, the ones he dubbed the Angels of Death.

He never told us how that happened. All he told us was that the Angels of Death were brainwashed Pasdúnami who were forced to kill their own kind against their will, but only when given the order, mostly to family members who were Pasdúnami themselves. They were founded three years after the secret police was established. He was also responsible for brainwashing Jacob and having him kill Fedora, making himself the real murderer and Jacob as the scapegoat. Cali's parents were killed four months later. Eleven months before Fedora, the parents of the mysterious girl named Janice Campbell were killed in the explosion with her status unknown. The secret police hunted her down for years, as she evaded them every time, even outside of Nova Vega.

That was not possible. No one could escape from the country and survive outside of it for that long. Unless...it was possible that she had the ability to travel to different dimensions. Either that, or there might be a civilization outside of Nova Vega after all. Either way, she was the first one to ever escape the secret police and stay alive.

Fueled by anger and hate, with his eyes burning in rage, teeth clinched together, and arms shaking in fury, Kent tore parts of the warehouse interior pillars and materialized them into a sword and a gun. He grabbed the sword with his right hand, while grabbing the gun with his left. He readied his battle stance. He looked at me and communicated telepathically, *Go! Get your stuff and get yourself and the group out of here!*

I was afraid for him at first, but I had to trust him, nodding in agreement. Using my telekinesis, I levitated the bags and grabbed hold of Riley, Gabriella, Ferenc, and Cali in the form of a hug. Picturing the purple-walled living room in my mind, the five of us teleported to the one place the secret police wouldn't think to find us: The Truman Residence.

XXIV- Phoebe Truman

Escaping from the secret police was easy, especially since we learned that they have the Angels of Death at their side, all the more reason we needed to run. For all we knew, they could've arrived with them and Rex the whole time, and we didn't realize it. It was best not to take any chances. I didn't blame Gabriella for worrying about her brother since he had to stay behind to hold off Rex.

And to make matters worse, Riley was angry, eyebrows tightening together as he punched the walls. The divorce façade really affected him badly. It took about five minutes to get our ally to calm down. Fedora's death was one thing, but Tess's death hit Riley really hard. I felt sad for him, but at the same time I was furious and pissed at the government, the secret police, all of the cohorts that caused us so much pain and misery all of our lives.

Anyway, two minutes of mourning his mother, after calming down from his rage, Riley gave me the paper containing the address Hestia told him to teleport his pets to earlier. Since Ferenc and I only had one cat, Beet had to go there. With us away from Nova Vega, she needed someone to look after her. Both of us wouldn't be there for her for a long time. Until our return, she would need a substitute caretaker. She rubbed against my legs, meowing like a kitten. It was sad that I had to leave her with Hestia for a long while, and I was going to miss her a lot. But I needed to remain strong for her sake. Looking at the address on the paper, and with a single touch on my cat's head, I teleported Beet to 400 Roth Ave. Philadelphia, PA, whatever that place was.

After my cat was teleported, Ferenc and I noticed Gabriella collapsed on the wooden floor on both knees. She had a stunned expression on her face. We were going to ask her what was wrong, but she jumped up from the floor and attempted to rush out the door. I held the door, and my brother used telekinesis to freeze her.

"Let me go!" she yelled. "Kent is in danger!"

"You can't leave!" said Ferenc. "The secret police and the government would be expecting that. If you leave, they'll find us and kill us."

"But Kent…"

"He can take care of himself. And if he gets killed, Cali will bring him back," he looked at Cali, who was sitting on the blue couch alongside Riley. "Right?"

"That's another thing! She'll die, too! We'll all die! That's why I need to get Kent! It's not safe for him anymore!"

"Then leave him!"

Ferenc's yell startled even Riley and Cali, and he continued, "We escaped with our lives! Now, we have to wait until the commotion dies down for us to leave Nova Vega!"

"We can't leave without him! Without him, I'll have no one by my side! He's my brother, and he's the only family alongside Riley I have left!"

"I'm sorry, but we all have to make sacrifices no matter how cruel they are."

Ferenc cancelled the effect and walked to his bedroom. Gabriella, too heartbroken to even talk, fell on her knees once more. I held her close to my chest as she started crying, taking my brother's words to heart. I felt sorry for her, but I was not the only one. Riley and Cali felt the same way. While she was crying, I was angry. My brother didn't understand the fact that Gabriella's love for her family was strong. Attachment may lead to jealousy, but only when it involves the dead. But for the living, it depends. Ferenc, having abandonment issues was bad enough, but being cynical about Kent's fate based on our choices was really uncalled for. If what Gabriella said was true, then her brother could be in big trouble. For the time being, we had to remain in hiding, Kent could take care of himself, hopefully he could survive.

***

For the next three days, while waiting on Kent to return, or some word to reveal his fate, his cousin Riley needed to find a way to entertain himself. I let him watch some dystopian movies, while Cali read *Divergent* on the couch. Apart from her, Riley's favorite genre was dystopia, as he would tell me later on that he wanted to protect the animals and the environment around us. It was good to know she was enjoying it, but I would hate to imagine what her reaction would be once she planned to read *Allegiant*. I'd read all of the books, and I knew how they turned out in the end. But it was wise not to tell her. She wouldn't want to hear any spoiler alerts. Ferenc, on the other hand, was calling our mother's friend to get an airplane that could lead us out of Nova Vega. It took those three days to get the approval, but we managed to get plane tickets. But not for Kent, as my brother said, because according to him, our friend was beyond saving and must be allowed to die. To get out of my depression, and vent out my anger, I changed the channel on the television in the living room, much to Riley's dismay, who was watching his favorite buddy sitcom called "The Misadventures of Reuel and Raymond." It was about a comedy duo that usually get into trouble with the law whenever they did something stupid, such as how to interact with the right woman, what the right decision in reality is, and part-time jobs.

110

As I flipped through the channels, Riley and I began fighting over the remote. Ferenc, Gabriella, and Cali saw the whole thing and tried to break up the fight, which resulted in the television getting changed from channel to channel. It lasted for thirty seconds, until it flipped to the Nova Vegan International News. The anchorman and anchorwoman were both Morphers. Their names were Peter Snow and Pamela Matthews, and they were actually elderly people who were expected to retain their young age. They were planning on going into retirement twenty years back, but the government bribed them to stay, lest they get sentenced to death and have their bodies cast out of Nova Vega.

Snow had short, light-brown hair, violet eyes, tan skin, and wore a black business suit with a blue tie, glasses, and brown business shoes. Matthews had black hair reaching down shoulder-length, blue eyes, brown skin, and wore a black business suit with a red tie and black high-heel shoes. I was impressed by their young appearances, but I did feel sorry for them, being threatened to be cast out of Nova Vega; execution is both unfair and messed up. Though they looked healthy, Anchorman Snow coughed on occasion, either he was ill, or dying, or both. I wouldn't blame them for wanting to retire, but at the same time, I felt ill having to learn that they weren't allowed to retire, lest they get killed.

"Three days ago, there was an uprising between Rosewood High School and the Nova Vegan Secret Police," said Anchorwoman Matthews. "The death causalities were 17 students, 3 teachers, Principal White, and 30 enforcers. The uprising ended with the captain restraining the school body and placing them under arrest."

"Sources say that the young man by the name of Kent Bernard, son of Hypnotist Patriarch and lawyer Jacob Bernard, was responsible for this act of treason and was placed into government custody," said Anchorman Snow. "There will be a public execution behind St. Paul United Methodist Church tomorrow morning."

Tomorrow morning?! That was terrible! There had to be a way to stop the execution and save Kent. And I wasn't the only one desperate. Gabriella was the same way. She snatched the remote from my hand and turned off the T.V. She looked at all four of us and said, "We have to save Kent."

"Oh, not this again!" Ferenc shouted in anger, being insensitive again, but now ungrateful. "I get it! You want to save your brother, but I told you three days ago, we all have to make sacrifices no matter how cruel they can be!"

"Maybe *you* don't care what happens to Kent, but I do!" I scolded. "And it's not just him! It's about all of Nova Vega, including Wayne County!"

"No, *you* said Kent was important!"

"I never said that! I said it's not just him! Right now, he's the top priority!"

"You can't save everyone!"

"Because you won't let us!"

111

"Because I trust myself better than I do everyone else!"

"Stop it!" Cali screamed, as she got between us. "Stop fighting! Damn!" She looked at Ferenc with a mixture of disappointment and anger. "Ever since you came back to life, thanks to me, *you've* been trying to hold everyone, including Gabriella back! Since when did you become our father?!"

"Since my parents placed me in charge of the house and my sister! And even if they are still alive, I'm not going to bother looking for them either! They told me that I'm in charge until they return!"

Crossing her arms over her chest, she berated, "Then, your parents would be ashamed of you! If that were them in Kent's position right now, what would you do?!"

"That's different! I would've saved them!"

"Then, what are you so afraid of?! That we're going to wind up like Fedora, Tess, and my parents?! Yeah, your parents placed you in charge, but they never said you have the right to abuse your authority!"

"Well, Mom and Dad are not here right now! As long as I'm in charge, all of you have to abide by the rules of the house *my* way!" he looked at Gabriella, as his face reddened with anger. "Go to Phoebe's room, Gabriella! No meals for the rest of the day!" he looked at the rest of us. "And here's my curfew for the rest of you! You will get washed up and go to bed early tonight! We're leaving in the morning! Anyone who leaves the house will face the consequences! Is that clear?!"

His voice was so loud that almost all of the neighborhood could hear him. He didn't care. It's like he wanted the neighborhood to hear him, let them know that he was the boss under our parents' roof. Gabriella rushed into my room, crying hard enough to not want to leave. Riley did the same, except he wasn't sad. He was angry. Before he went to my room with his cousin, he stopped halfway upstairs and looked at him one last time, telling him that he was "a fricking asshole!" He slammed the door with a lot of rage built up in him. Who could blame him?

I had to agree with Gabriella, Cali, and Riley. Ever since Ferenc became the man of the house and returned from the dead, he wasn't the same. It's like he let his resurrection go to his head. If I was in Kent's shoes, would my own brother leave me to die, or save me? This was the one question I didn't want to ask him. Knowing him, he would choose the former. Selfish jackass. I glared daggers at him with a cold expression on my face and scolded him, "Real mature of you, Ferenc. I liked you better before you were dead."

His face snapped in my direction, gawking before I went into my room. Cali, who shook her head at him feeling ashamed, came along with me. I only said that to him because his authority over the house turned from better to worse. The man who liked to startle me and laugh when giving the smile of a child and was less cautious than usual was gone. He was not the Ferenc I once knew. He was more cynical than ever before.

***

Later at night, when Ferenc went to bed, I woke Gabriella up. She was a light sleeper anyway, and so was Cali. Riley, however, was a heavy sleeper. So, Cali pounced on him, waking him up at a bad time, at least in his case. He got irritated when waking up. He would've slept on the couch with either Gabriella, or Cali, but his loud snoring would've kept them up all night.

Opening the door leading downstairs and going halfway down, the coast was already clear. I went back to my room and said to Gabriella, Riley, and Cali, "We're going to bust Kent out of prison and save him from execution."

"But Ferenc said—"

I interrupted Gabriella and said, "I don't care what my brother says. Even since he came back from the dead, he started caring more about himself than he does everyone else, including Kent. After what he did for my brother, this is the thanks the former gets? Now, the latter only gives a shit about what's been going on in his life and no one else's," I said looking at Cali, blushing embarrassingly. "Forgive my potty mouth."

"No worries," Cali responded with a smile on her face. "It's all good. And for once, I'm glad you did. Your brother's a jerk anyway. He believes in being selfish first and being selfless later, or in his case, selfless never."

"Touché," I looked at Gabriella. "Where do they usually keep criminals?"

"Nova Vegan Prison," she answered. "It used to be Wayne County Jail before it was renovated into such after the war. And people can't use powers when inside a cell, or in the interrogation room, or even the execution ground."

"Then, we have to be careful and not get caught, as well as keep our minds closed at all cost."

"Are you saying...?"

I interrupted Riley and answered, "Yep. We teleport outside of prison, sneak inside without getting caught, break Kent out, and get back here before Ferenc knows we vanished."

"What about the other prisoners?"

"Well, presuming Seifer, Mark, Valeda, and Asteria are alive, if they survived, we'll break them and the survivors involved in that uprising out, too."

There was a long pause at first, but after a while, Gabriella knew that it would be the right thing to do. Riley and Cali decided to go along with the plan, too. It was settled. Before the crack of dawn, we were to save Kent and the survivors of the uprising, bring him to the Truman Residence, and leave Nova Vega. The rescue mission was about to be tough, but it would be worth the shot.

XXV- Kent Bernard

Three days earlier- With a sword and gun at hand, I was ready to confront the man inside the warehouse that I once called my uncle. He levitated the tranquilizer darts from the unconscious bodies of his officers and fused them together to forge a sword. It had a gray blade with a green hilt. I felt nothing but hatred toward him, and he was out for my blood. We clashed our swords, beginning our duel to the death.

The battle was brutal, like roaring thunder before the lightning struck the land. It was as vicious as wolves fighting over their meat in the forest. I managed to dodge Rex's sword, but it already gave me a gushing cut on my chest from the bottom of the right side to the top of the left, groaning in pain as a result. Had it gone any deeper than that, he would've sliced my heart and lungs in half, killing me instantly. Still, I was already bleeding, and I snarled in rage.

As he cut me in the chest, I shot him from the right cheek to the tragus, antihelix, auricle of his right ear. He screamed in agony when he felt the bullet fly deep into the skin and near the interior. Blood spew out, dripping from his hand as he covered it. I teleported in front of him and attempt to strike him down, but he blocked the sword with his. It was difficult for him to wield it with his left hand. He didn't want to experience more blood loss. Wait a minute. Why didn't he use his healing ability like he did with Cass? Something was not right. Unless...that's it! He was healing himself!

I knew what I had to do. I needed to cut off Rex's right arm. Unfortunately, he smacked the sword from my hand as a counterattack and pushed me to the wall with his telekinesis. I lost my grip on the gun, too, before falling on the ground. Trying to get up, I focused on him in an attempt to punch him in the face. But as I teleported over to him, Sirena, who watched the fight alongside the Emmerich Brothers, did the same in the same spot. It happened again when I teleported behind him. Her perception grew the last time we met, making her just as dangerous as the Emmerich Brothers. And she and I had a teleportation fight when my attempts to get close to the captain were foiled.

Above him, Sirena pinned me to the floor with her knee on my neck hard, causing me to cough roughly as the back of my skull nearly cracked on the concrete floor, where the metal would've been earlier, if not for Cali's powers. My vision was becoming blurry as I tried to teleport again, but to no avail. I was choking; choking, and dying. With some vision left, I saw the Emmerich Brothers looming over me as well. They held me down by the arms so I wouldn't escape, hence my attempt to grab my enemy's leg. And to make certain I wouldn't make another attempt to teleport while pinned down, Sirena knocked me out with a single punch. Everything in my view went dark.

***

There was the room again, and the woman resembling a teenager from my earlier dream was in some sort of training room with the man that loomed over her last time observing the whole thing. Instead of the light-green operation cloak, she was in a purple combat uniform with black leather boots.

There were five others with her. One of them was a tall man with short, black hair, blue eyes, and fair skin, whom she fell in love with and vice versa. The second man was of Korean descent; black hair, brown eyes, fair skin. He told his life stories to inspire his friends. The third person, and second woman, was Hispanic with long, dark-red hair, green eyes, and she had the most amazing singing voice. The fourth person, and third man, was African, hence his black hair, brown eyes, and dark skin, and he had an amazing sense of humor, showing his friends that even in tough times, there was always a way to brighten their day. The last person, and third woman, was British with reddish-blonde hair, hazel eyes, and fair skin, and known for her no-nonsense personality and making sure they stayed focused on the training during the course.

They were all in combat training in a city-structured simulation, but the third man was injured, and the second woman healed him. The third woman disguised herself as one of the animatronic mannequins and caught them off guard. The second man protected the third man and second woman by tackling the animatronic mannequins. With the first woman and first man's help, the same third woman combined her animation powers with theirs to create the metallic army and defeat the mannequins.

The man dressed as a pastor with his head still in the shadow congratulated the six combatants and told them to "get some rest." Before the Pasdúnami trainees left for their rooms, he said to them, "May the Maker protect you all."

***

I woke up, and there I was, back in jail; the same cell as before— same bad smell, same bed, and same graffiti on the ceiling from my first time. Only that time, I was a prisoner of war, thanks to Rex, Sirena, and the Emmerich Brothers. How long was I out? I did not know. Then, I heard a voice coming from my right but on the other side of the bricked wall. "Kent? Is that you?" the voice said.

115

My eyes widened in surprise as I looked to the right. I knew that voice.

"Seifer?" I asked. "You're here? But how?"

"The Captain of the Secret Police arrested me and the survivors a few hours ago after you and the Aurora left," he answered.

"But you're not going to believe who that captain is. It was Rex Weston, Riley's father, or should I say ex-father thanks to revealing his true nature in front of us."

"Riley's dad is the captain of that damn secret police?"

"Unfortunately, yes. He betrayed his family to the government and was responsible for the secret police's foundation after he murdered Aunt Tess. He even used my father to murder my mother."

"He did what?! Why would he do that?!"

"Apparently my parents and Riley's parents were part of some rebel group with a mission to free Nova Vega."

"And that's when your ex-uncle betrayed them and joined the government?"

"Yes. By the way, where are Mark, Valeda, and Asteria? Are they safe?"

"Yes. And is Phoebe safe?"

"Yes, she's safe."

"Good. Glad to hear it."

Before we had a chance to talk further, there was banging on the jail cell. It was Officer White and he was not in the best of moods. My guess was that he heard about the death of his brother, and he blamed me for it, even though Rex was the one who killed him. Not even reasoning with him would do any good. Why would he? He worked for the Nova Vegan government. And nothing I, or the Aurora could do would ever convince him otherwise, evidence or no evidence.

Jumping off the top bunk, I walked over to him willingly, and when he opened the cell, he placed me in handcuffs. While escorting me to wherever I was going, he said to me bitterly. "You have messed with the system for the last time, Bernard. You got my brother killed, and the chancellor will have a word with you in the interrogation room. She will expect you to tell her everything. Once a juvenile delinquent always a juvenile delinquent."

***

The metallic interrogation room had a silver table and two silver chairs, an overhead light at the center of the ceiling, and a one-way window at my right. Like the cells in Nova Vegan Prison, the room was power-proof. Why would they put me in handcuffs if the entire room was already power-proof? Paranoia, perhaps. That's what corruption can do to a person when running a country.

Speak of the devil, and she doth appear. A recognizable figure came from the door. Fading red hair reaching the neck, gray eyes, fair skin, pink lips, thirty-three years old- wearing a purple business suit with a skirt reaching below the knees, a red tie, and black high-heel shoes. It was the first time I'd met the Nova

116

Vegan Chancellor herself: Cyria Jelen. After hearing about what she did and reading about what she had done; from ordering the no-longer secret manhunt for the Pasdúnami to the deaths of my mother, Aunt Tess, Cali's parents, and many others. She also enforced unfair laws, like job restrictions based on Tribes, refusal of jobs for students under college graduate-level, and condemning lower-class citizens. How I learned about her age? According to the article I read the other day, she was twenty-eight during Janice's disappearance and her parents' deaths. I didn't trust the chancellor already. Her wicked smile told me she didn't care if I was full of bitterness and hostility toward her. I felt like I wanted to strangle her to death while I was in handcuffs, twitching my fingers in anger, ready to use my powers, unblocked, if given the chance.

"Kent Tavi Bernard," she said in her British Accent, being of British ancestry perhaps.

She took out her holographic device- a metallic hemisphere with a tiny component that showed any recordings, newspapers, and other sources of information with the touch of the black button at the front. Chancellor Jelen placed it in the middle of the table, showing my records about the past before continuing, "You have been a nuisance to the government for the past three years, haven't you?"

"That's what happens when it treats its citizens like crap and enforces unfair laws," I said in a bitter tone.

"Hence robberies and shoplifting. And three years back, you noticed a surveillance camera for the first time. But a little tip for next time: Never look in environmental spots alone. Why do you think my cohort's police found your Little John's hiding spot?"

Glaring at her, my mind was burning with so much hostility, I responded, "There wasn't surveillance at the hiding spot."

"But there was one in the hover motorcycle. Didn't think about that, did you?"

Her gloating expression made me even madder. She continued, "Didn't think so," her expression turned to anger as her eyebrows drew together with her smile fading into a frown as she scowled at me. "But you should know that every Robin Hood must have his Prince John and Sheriff of Nottingham. This isn't a legend. This is reality, and in the real world, it's either respect authority, or pay the price."

"You and Rex killed my mother!" I growled like a ravaged wolf. "You both used my father to poison her!"

"Jacob was a guard dog in our eyes. Rex knew what he was doing. If he couldn't kill his own sister with his own hands, then he would have to do it through another."

"But Rex is a Pasdúnamis! By letting him do as he please, you, too, committed heresy!"

"True, I became a hypocrite by committing heresy, breaking the very law that the government established, but for every law, exceptions must sometimes be made! Like Rex said before, *'Sometimes, you have to fight fire with fire!'* To establish true peace, freedom must cease to exist!" she calmed herself. "Take away that freedom, everything becomes dictatorship. And the one thing about dictatorship is that it can be reasonable."

"Until dictatorship lets power go to its holder's head."

"Just like your mother, always worrying about what would happen to the world around you."

"Phoebe did the same thing, and she did it for the right reason! She worried for the people she loves, and she was devastated when her brother was killed! That action, as well as my determination to fight back gave her hope! And if it weren't for Cali, Phoebe's hope would never have gotten stronger than ever, and Ferenc would've remained dead!"

"Which he should've, and rightfully deserved it. Too bad you and Cali were too late getting to sweet Fedora's corpse on time. I have to admit, I did find you crying for your precious mommy pathetic. Death happens all the time, and whether it's timely or not, it has to happen, even if my government has to enforce death upon my enemies."

"So, now what? You're gonna force death upon me, too?"

She chuckled for a little bit and responded, "I'd rather not. Instead, I'm going to make you an offer."

Her words left me surprised, but not in the way I hoped. "Tell me where the Aurora is, and in return, I'll spare your life. That, and you'll be joining the government with open arms."

That offer was like making a pact with the Devil, and Chancellor Jelen was the Devil. How could I even help her if I didn't know where the Aurora was located? The Aurora left before I fought Rex. Clenching my fist at the thought of what my enemies planned to do to them, I glared at her with rage in my brain and fire in my eyes, answering her with bitter hostility, "Fuck you!"

Her expression turned from prideful back to anger. She stood up, walked around the table, and looked directly into my eyes as she bended down. That made me feel a little uneasy as my stomach dropped, but at the same time, glaring daggers at her, I was defiant.

"You can't protect your friends and family forever, Kent," she said. "You have three days before the trial. That will give you plenty of time to give me your real answer."

She looked at the door, and Officer White came in. The cruel chancellor stood up, looking back at me with another wicked smile, and said, "And don't get any ideas about praying to the Maker. A God who is protective of His children doesn't deserve to be a God among them. Thanks to *you*, He can't protect Nova Vega anymore, let alone you. Because of *you*, your God has forsaken you and this country. The Nova Vegan government is your God now."

Bitch. You know nothing about the Maker. That's what I would've said to her, but I learned that day that she didn't care what happened to Nova Vega. She tortured them, because she expected too much from us. She killed them, because they were nothing but a means to an end to her, or they knew too much in her eyes. Rex was not the only enemy I needed to deal with. Cyria Jelen was also the enemy that I needed to stop for good. But as long as I was in prison, I was powerless.

See you in three days, Chancellor.

XXVI- Kent Bernard

Three days passed and my hatred toward my enemies grew stronger, but at the same time, so did my fear for everyone in Nova Vega. It didn't matter what I did. Even if I didn't know where the Aurora was, I was going to die either way. And when morning came, I was about to stand trial for my criminal acts against the Nova Vegan government. But Chancellor Jelen still expected me to join her and betray the Aurora, which would also mean to betray all of Nova Vega, if it was on our side of course. Before going to court, I was forced to wear an orange jumpsuit with a pair of black boots.

And once again, Officer White escorted me. He still hated me, as the hostility in his eyes told me. He still blamed me for what happened to his brother, and I almost felt sorry for him. Like I said, he couldn't be reasoned with. As long as my criminal records remained intact, nothing could ever convince him to change his opinions of me, not even the truth. If Principal White was alive, or came back from the dead, would he be relieved, or would he expect me to stay away from them? I would never know. And you know who the judge of the court was?

***

Azuriah Devin, the first Judge President of Nova Vega. He had greying-black hair, light-green eyes, fair skin, full beard, and wore a black robe like any other judge of the court. He wore a purple tie to go along with his judge's outfit. Before he founded the title, he was the Supreme Court Judge of Nova Vega. Five years back, he became the first Judge President after Mussolitler's death. And the worse part, he was the patriarch of the Element Manipulator Tribe.

As for Cyria, he stood at Rex, Sirena, and the Emmerich Brothers' side as part of the Nova Vegan Jury, which made me feel uneasy and subtly hostile. Even in court, Cyria was the matriarch of the Telepath Tribe. Ironically, she actually gave me a choice. No dictator would ever give their enemies a choice. They would make them do something against their will. Should they disobey, their enemies would face the consequences, no matter how evil and cruel. While she ran everything in Nova Vega, Judge President Devin supervised its laws, declare them constitutional or not, and decided the fate of his enemies.

The courtroom was massive with gray walls, and two sides of the pew style gallery were behind me as I stood in the criminal circle. The jury box was next to me and the huge judge's bench was in front of me. It felt like Hell merged with Heaven, giving me a reason to hate the government more. I gave the judge president an angry scowl. I hated him just as much as I hated Chancellor Jelen, Captain Rex, Sirena, and the Emmerich Brothers combine. And with the sound of his black gavel hitting the block, Judge President Devin spoke, "The Nova Vegan Supreme Court is now in session," he looked down at me. "Kent Tavi Bernard, you have committed crimes of thievery, sympathy for the lower class and heretics, and treason. Defiance against the Nova Vegan government is an unforgivable crime which is punishable by death. How do you plead?"

"Not guilty," I answered, causing the Emmerich Brothers to drop their jaws and Sirena widening her eyes. "Yes, I committed those crimes, but for the right reason. The real criminals are Chancellor Jelen, Captain Rex, Sirena, and the Emmerich Brothers. Jelen ordered the eradication of the Pasdúnami, the solution for Nova Vega's salvation. Rex murdered my mother Fedora through my father Jacob, who was a sleeper agent, and many others. Sirena tried to kill me and Phoebe with the Emmerich Brothers' help. Not only that, but they manipulated the laws to plague fear on its citizens."

"But the uprising at Rosewood High School was all your doing, Mr. Bernard. The government saw and heard your speech, and Cyria told me everything. She also requested that I let you live, if you tell us where the radical group called the Aurora is. Do so, and you'll be free and join the government."

There was no other point. Even if I did know where my friends, sister, and cousin were, I would never rat them out. I was about to die either way. I looked at the chancellor, knowing that she had the capability to read people's minds. Since we weren't at the police station, it was time to tell them the truth.

"It doesn't matter what I tell you," I rebuked, as I glared daggers at Judge President Devin. "Even if I did know where my friends were, I would never tell you. You'll end up sentencing me to death either way."

"He's telling the truth," Jelen answered, as she gave me a disappointing glare. "He doesn't know where they are," she looked at the judge president, who looked at her in return. "And he's very perceptive."

"Very well," said the cruel judge president, looking back at me. "Kent Tavi Bernard, I hereby sentence you to death and execution through hanging at dawn."

My stomach dropping in horror, I knew that it was going to happen. The judge even declared Rex to be my executioner. At the back of St. Paul United Methodist Church, I was to be hanged until dead. If I struggled, the firing squad would finish the job. That was how executions worked, if the executed survived. And before dawn, I sadly wished Seifer a Happy Birthday. He'd turned sixteen. The birthday wish was more than enough for him, even though I heard him crying. He feared that it would be his last birthday and I felt the same way as I closed my eyes, tears draining from my eyes.

***

Dawn came, and my execution was coming. There was no telling what would happen to Nova Vega after Seifer; standing behind me, and I were gone. His only crime was treason. My sister, cousin, and my friends, however, would be devastated, but at the same time, outraged as I would become a martyr to them. Would it be for the good of the country? Or would it spill more blood and violence; which could result in the end of the world as we knew it?

But Seifer and I weren't the only ones about to face a death sentence. And in front of us was a teenage girl three inches taller than me. Her short, dark-brown hair hugged the sides of her face and her brown eyes brightened her pale skin. A slightly horizontal scar showed on her right arm above the elbow.

The gallows awaited us behind St. Paul United Methodist Church on a dark cloudy morning with thunderstorms, but no rain. It was seven feet from the bottom of the stairs to the top, and there were three nooses installed on the hanging bar, held by two 8' tall poles, suspending over three trapdoors. The teenage girl took the left rope noose, Seifer took the right, and I took the middle. Rex was at the lever next to teenage girl. There was a big crowd, shouting with those who wanted us dead, while the rest wanted us alive. I didn't blame the latter. Even I didn't want to die, but I didn't resist. All was lost, and hope faded from the last minutes of my life. Seifer's family knew he didn't deserve to die either. His father, Mr. Valentine, had a sad expression on his face as he held Mrs. Valentine tight while she cried in his arms. Seifer's sisters and brother shed tears also, looking up at their older brother in defeat.

The teenage girl at my left glared at me with anger in her eyes and shouted, "Hey, man!" She caught my hopeless attention with despair in my eyes. "Why are you just standing there?! You escaped the cruel law before! Don't be a coward. Save yourself!"

"Be quiet!" Seifer scolded from my right, catching both of our attention. "He's doing what is right in his heart! Have you no sense of morality?!"

A martyr, or an example of defiance, it didn't matter. This was it. I closed my eyes as a single tear came down from my right eye. My death was approaching. Soon, I would be joining my mother. I waited four years to see her again. Also, I would meet Aunt Tess for the first time. Then again, I don't know where I'd go to after death. My fate was for the Maker's to decide. Not the Nova Vegan government. Not Rex. Not Chancellor Jelen. Not Judge President Devin. Only the Maker.

122

Gabriella, Riley, look after one another. I thought. *Ferenc, when I first met you, I knew you were a pain in the ass, even when you were trying to protect your sister, and I didn't blame you. Take good care of her. Cali,...Phoebe,...I love you.*

Once Rex pulled the lever, my feet couldn't feel anything. But something happened as the trapdoors opened. There were gunshots, and, to my confusion, my neck didn't snap. What the hell was going on?

XXVII- Phoebe Truman

Before the crack of dawn, Gabriella, Riley, Cali, and I teleported out of the Truman Residence and reappeared in Downtown Goldsboro. Before we did, Bernard-Weston Cousins and I changed out of our school uniforms. I wore a gray short-sleeve shirt with a black waistcoat, blue shorts, black gloves, and black boots; glad to not be in the same uniform every school day. Riley was back in his usual outfit, the same one he wore during Fedora's funeral, both sad and happy, as he told me later on. Gabriella wore a white shirt with green short sleeves, black pants, and brown combat boots, overjoyed to get out of her feminine clothes for once. Overall, the four of us wore black hooded cloaks to hide our appearances from the public, as the government might recognize who we were by now. Precaution was everything in a rescue mission.

Kent's execution was only seven minutes away. There was no time to lose. We had to get to Nova Vegan Prison, a massive gray building with a black roof, and rescue him from his untimely and unfair death. We stayed hidden in the shadows through alleyways and between buildings; the post office and massive white marble courthouse. Upon our arrival, the prison was guarded. Riley reached into his jacket pocket, and to my surprise, and Gabriella's, he had Newt. We thought he was teleported to the shelter's location with the rest of his pets. Riley had a plan to infiltrate Nova Vegan Prison.

With four minutes left, there was no time to argue between the Bernard-Weston Cousins, especially over how Riley didn't bother to send his newt to the safe haven with the rest of the newts and his pets. For once, Gabriella was glad that he brought his newt along and used her telekinesis to levitate Newt, throwing him at one of the guards' faces. Upon seeing him, he screamed bloody murder, alerting his partner. We silently chuckled at the guard's reaction to the sudden appearance of Riley's pet newt. The second officer took out his baton, getting ready to whack Newt into jelly. The first officer slightly shook in fear as the newt crawled to his chest, and at the last second, Gabriella levitated the little salamander away right on cue. When she did, the second officer hit the first officer hard in the chest, making him groan in pain as he clutched the painful spot. Newt came back to Riley and crawled back into his pocket.

Cali rushed to the officers, took their batons, and knocked them out cold, while they were distracted. Waving at me, Gabriella, and Riley, we entered the lion's den; the Nova Vegan Prison, after we hid the unconscious officers in the bushes.

***

There were only three minutes before the execution, and to our luck, all of the stations were empty. It seemed that law enforcement went to the execution grounds to await the accused. And I was right. Coming from the right side was the escort, and the four of us rushed and ducked under the main station. It was a white desk with filing cabinet on both sides, a computer on the left side, and a calendar in the middle with a nameplate at the very front. Cali covered my mouth after I almost yelled in pain from Riley accidentally having his right foot on my foot.

Slightly raising up from beneath the crawling space, we noticed the secret police officers escorting three prisoners. We didn't know who the teenage girl was, but behind her, much to our eye-widening relief, it was Kent, hanging his head. Looking behind him…oh, no! Seifer! He was on the execution list, too!

The four of us needed to do something and fast. If we didn't rescue them, they would die. So, we waited until they left the building to follow them. And as I opened the door, I caught Gabriella looking in awe. What was she looking at? What about Kent? Gabriella grabbed some sort of disc that was labelled "Classified" from the same desk we were hiding under. I said to her in irritation, "Gabriella, this is not the time to browse around. We have to save Kent, Seifer, and whoever that girl is."

"Coming," she said, as the four of us ran out the building.

***

With only one minute and thirty seconds left, the execution was coming. The four of us watched from the crowd as Kent, Seifer, and the teenage woman took their positions at the gallows. Rex, smiling cruelly, was eager to end the life of his own nephew; if he'd ever acknowledged him as such. I glared at him in disgust and didn't want to just stand there and watch them die. Too many people died at the hands of the government. Tenacious enough to put an end to it all, I picked up a rock next to my right foot and materialized it into a revolver, aiming at the very man responsible for our pain and misery.

Then, a hand grabbed mine, and I looked to my right. To my eye-widening surprise, it was Mark with Valeda. He placed his finger on his lips, signaling me to stay quiet and look at Rex. All I saw were his hazel eyes. But my eyes widened in surprise, and it hit me. I looked at the both of them, and they nodded. Oh, my goodness. That was Asteria. She may have had the same color eyes as Rex, but when Mark and Valeda nodded, it all made since.

But what happened to Rex? And how did Mark, Valeda, and Asteria escape the arrest? There was no time to ask. The execution was in forty seconds according to the clock tower behind the gallows. Mark looked at Riley and Gabriella, signaling them to pick up their own rock and materialize it into revolvers, too. While staying among the crowd, the three of us aimed at the ropes above the three accused people's heads. My heart was racing in fear. Fear that I would either miss the rope, or kill either one of them by mistake. With no time for a Plan B, it was a risk we would all have to take. The hanging was approaching in 3...2...1...pulled the lever. That was the signal, and without hesitation, the three of us shot at the ropes, freeing Kent, Seifer, and the teenage girl from execution.

Unfortunately, the sound of gunshots alerted and frightened the crowd, and Asteria morphed back into her normal form. Gabriella, Riley, Cali, and I, after removing our hoods, ran to Kent and hugged him in relief. We did the same for Seifer. Mark, Valeda, and Asteria came on over as well. Even Seifer's family, expressing tears of relief and joy, came. In fact, they wouldn't stop suffocating him. And it was a good thing they were open-minded people. After all, Mr. and Mrs. Valentine were the leaders of the Teleporter Tribe, which Seifer told me about. Mr. Valentine had greying-brown hair and hazel eyes, and Mrs. Valentine had strawberry-blonde hair and blue eyes. And thanks to Asteria, the handcuffs were removed from the three former prisoners.

Seifer's parents, who brought us over to near the church away from the fearful crowd, were friends with Cali's parents before they died. We were told that should anything happen to Joshua and Sarah, then Mr. and Mrs. Valentine would be their successors. Despite being in different districts in Wayne County, they remained in contact. To our surprise, they were part of the rebel cell alongside my parents and Kent's parents and revealed the reason behind Rex's betrayal. It turned out that Rex was telling the truth back at the warehouse, but the rest of the truth was not told. Mr. and Mrs. Valentine explained another part of the rebel cell's agenda in freeing the country from tyranny.

While it sought to bring peace between the Pasdúnami and the Dúnami, instead, Rex wanted dominance over the Dúnami. He wanted them to feel the same pain as the Pasdúnamis Tribe when they were labelled heretics, even though not everyone of the Dúnamis Civilization was evil. When the rebel cell discovered his treachery, he was excommunicated, but not before he kidnapped Tess as his last act of high treason. After he brainwashed Jacob and had Tess, Fedora, and Cali's parents killed, Mr. and Mrs. Valentine became the leaders of both the rebel cell and the Teleporter Tribe. Even the rebel cell has Dúnami among the group.

Then, it hit us. Rex mentioned something about a disc. Could it be the disc that Gabriella took from Nova Vegan Prison? We weren't sure. We needed to take a look at it just to be sure.

"We have to get to my house," I said. "If this is the disc that's meant to be delivered to the central broadcast network, then it's not safe at this time."

"She's right," said Rinoa, who had strawberry-blonde hair and fierce hazel eyes, which made me like her already, and is the second eldest child of the Valentine Family. "Right now, our top priority is to rally Wayne County and fight back against the government."

"No one is going to do anything!" Sirena screamed in rage, appearing from the crowd alongside the Emmerich Brothers. Sirena yelled, "You all have defied the government for the last time!"

"And you're a disgrace to the Teleporter Tribe!" said Mr. Valentine. "Teleportation is meant to be used to help people, not for personal gain!"

"Times have changed, old man," she gave a cruel smile. "It is time for the younger generation to take over. Chancellor Jelen gave me permission to execute the accomplices of the Aurora, and I will become the new matriarch of the Teleporter Tribe. So, who's the disgrace?"

Enraged, eyes glaring at Sirena, I dematerialized the revolver. And then used the wind to materialize a bow and arrows. I aimed my weapon at Sirena and stood in front of the Valentine Family.

"You will NOT harm a single hair on their heads!" I scolded. "You know nothing about disgrace! It's like Kent said before! The people of Nova Vega don't serve its government! It's the government that needs *us*! Without us, it is nothing!"

Kent used his telekinesis to rip a large chunk of wood from the other side of the crowd, grabbed it, and materialized it into a machine gun before aiming at Calvin.

"She's right!" he said. "Even if we, the Aurora, die at its hands, we will only become martyrs to the people!"

Mark, Valeda, and Asteria stood by our side. Mark, fierce and valiant, aimed his right hand at the gallows and manipulated all of the wood from it, catching the crowd's attention. Aiming his left hand, Mark manipulated the concrete of the parking lot and leaves of the bushes. Using both of his hands, he animated an army of Hardcore Soldiers with swords and guns made of concrete before being given a revolver by Gabriella. Valeda was given two revolvers by Cali. Asteria wielded Rex's sword-like baton.

"If you want to kill the Aurora!" said Asteria.

"Then, you'll have to kill us, too!" said Valeda.

"Yes, Mon!" said Mark. "*All* of us!"

I looked at Riley and said, "Riley, *you*, Gabriella, and Cali must bring the Valentine Family, Seifer, and the teenage girl back to the Truman Residence for safety."

Glaring daggers at me, the teenage girl said, "I do have a name, you know. It's Janice Campbell."

Our eyes widened in disbelief, and I asked, "*The* Janice Campbell, the missing girl who survived the explosion?"

"Which also killed my parents back at Virginia Beach thanks to the secret police assholes, yes."

She also told us that she had been on the run from the Nova Vegan government through dimensional travel for the last five years. What's insane is that she held a massive grudge against Chancellor Jelen for what she did to her parents. She trained in different worlds, which she would explain another time, preparing for the day that she would put an end to her enemy's tyranny. But the day after Labor Day, her assassination attempt failed, and she was arrested for it. She was also framed for the death of her parents.

Who could blame Janice for holding such a grudge? Framing a teenager was Jelen's last mistake. And that wasn't the worse part. The worse part was that, like Rex, Chancellor Jelen was a closeted Pasdúnamis. That was how Janice failed to end her life. She overpowered her before having her placed in prison.

After the Valentine Family, Janice, Gabriella, Riley, and Cali left, Kent, Mark, Valeda, Asteria, and I were the only ones to remain behind. This was it. It was a battle to win or die. But my stomach dropped in anxiety as things got complicated upon the arrival of the secret police. They were backed up by the police officers outside the group, moving in at Sirena and the Emmerich Brothers' side. Officer White, the new patriarch of the Morpher Tribe, sided with them, still oblivious, according to Kent, to the fact that Rex was the one who killed Principal White. His death clouded his mind, blackened his heart, and brought him to madness. To him, it was better to blame Kent than turn his back on the Captain of the Secret Police.

To our surprise, some of the citizens of Goldsboro, upon witnessing what happened at the gallows, and filled with determination after seeing the true colors of the government itself, went to our side. They had enough of its mistreatment, cruelty, manipulation, and over a century of deception. It was time for them to fight back, even if it cost them their lives. To our relief and joy, it was good to see that we made more allies. But the rest fled in fear, not wanting to see what they believed might become a bloodbath. Kent manipulated the concrete from most of the streets and materialized them into weapons; swords, guns, batons, and bows and arrows.

At the start of the battle, Kent and I hypnotized the Emmerich Brothers with all of our might, forcing them to attack each other like idiots from slapstick media. Officer White morphed into a secret police officer and attempted to shoot Kent in the heart. Mark managed to use two of his animated soldiers to block the bullets before attacking him and some of the police officers and secret police officers. He, Valeda, Asteria, and the citizens rushed into battle alongside the Hardcore Soldiers.

And for the first time, I developed the ability to read minds, hence unexpectedly hearing Sirena's thoughts. She was planning to kill Kent for not being there with her all those years ago. Talk about obsessive love. Before she had a chance to pull the trigger, I shot my arrow at the gun to disarm her, saving his life, leaving her outraged.

Then, I used telekinesis to bring the arrow back and fused all twelve of the arrows behind me together, forging a new sword. It was not like any regular sword. There was a red button at the bottom of the bronze hilt, and an arrowhead that was a tip of the silver blade. I called it Aduhim, the double female butterfly. It was unique, beautiful, and majestic.

I put the bow behind my back and gripped the sword tight with both hands. I looked at Kent and said to him in telepathy, *Go to 104 E Peter Street. That's my house. Leave Sirena with me.*

Alright, he thought back. *Be careful.*

I will.

He teleported to my house for safety and protection, while I looked back at Sirena, with fury in her eyes while clenching her teeth in rage. With determination on my face and burning in my eyes, I was ready for battle with my new sword at hand. But I wasn't the only one with a weapon. Sirena took out her very own sword-like baton. It was time for us to clash swords, and when we did, we teleported to different parts of Goldsboro, as long as our swords touched, while one of us thought about different locations to go to, or grabbing one another. Annoying as it might be, the battle had to go on.

***

The first place we teleported to was the roof of Wayne Memorial Hospital. Fierce, dangerous, and brutal, the sword-clashing was massively violent as if a thunderstorm mangled with a hurricane, spilling destruction in its path. We grabbed each other's wrists as we attempted to strike each other down, wrestling one another as we fixed our angry eyes directly at one another and clenched our teeth ferociously.

Not watching our step, we fell off the roof and teleported to the roof of Rosewood Middle School where I ended up with a large cut on my left arm, Sirena's right hand ended up with a cut that gushed blood. Groaning in pain, yet growling in rage, we clashed again as we dashed at one another. We teleported to what was left of Seymour Johnson Air Force Base next, right in front of the hanger. Thunder roared, and lightning flashed as things got out of hand. Blinded

129

by our fury, we punched each other in the face hard, giving one another a nosebleed.

Then as we clashed swords again, we teleported to the roof of Berkeley Mall before reappearing inside of the ruins of the UEC Theater to the Rosewood High School Football Field to Goldsboro Water Tower. We were equally matched the rest of the way, but Sirena fought dirty by punching me in the face again, causing me to lose balance and fall near the edge. She laughed at me. Aiming her sword-like baton at me, she yelled, "You think you know the Nova Vegan government, Truman! But guess what! You have no idea what we're capable of!"

"You have no idea what the Aurora is capable of!" I scolded, as I manipulated the metal from parts of the water tower.

She was going to stab me, but I grabbed her sword-like baton, even though the palm of my left hand was cut. Though I groaned in pain, it never stopped me from manipulating the metal. The metal swirled like a tornado mixed with a hurricane. The metal surrounded us, and Sirena showed fear in her eyes. Frozen in place, she was too jaw-dropping frightened to teleport away. She was right to be afraid, and I didn't plan to leave. Not until I finished what I started. Instead of finishing her off, I materialized the metal parts into chains. I manipulated them into trapping her and restraining her armed arm. And to make sure she wouldn't escape, I knocked her out cold with one punch.

With the battle won, it was time for me to go back to the Truman Residence. Ferenc was not going to be happy once he found out what I did. After all, he was insensitive and ungrateful, refusing to return Kent the favor of having him brought back from death. But I didn't care what he expected from me. Still, it was better to deal with him than dealing with Sirena. The consequences from him would be less tense and more severe.

XXVIII- Phoebe Truman

The good news was I made it back alive. But the bad news was that Ferenc was more than mad at me for disobeying him. Hey, I was only trying to help. Kent deserved to live. There was no way I was going to let him die. Not after everything he had done for all of Nova Vega. Not in Tribe Status, Class Status, etc., but as people. I knew what the outcome would be if he ended up becoming a martyr. It would spell disaster to the country, and evil would win. Well, okay. Not always, but sometimes, martyrdom promotes more conflicts and bloodbaths.

My brother and I argued in the living room for ten minutes, much to Mrs. Valentine's irritation and Gabriella's annoyance. Ferenc slapped me across the cheek hard, much to everyone's shock. My brother told me that because of me, "more blood will end up spilt." I punched him in the face in response, much to Janice's astonishment as she smiled, told him that it wouldn't have happened if he would just "listen to reason and stop being so negative." And finally, having had enough, Gabriella snapped as she got between us, "STOP IT!!!"

The sound of her voice startled all of us in the living room. Calming herself down, Gabriella took out the disc that she stole earlier and told us if we're done arguing, we needed to see what's so important about it. We reluctantly agreed, and she gave the disc to Seifer, who popped it in the DVD Player in front of the T.V. I turned on the television to see a woman who looked like an emotionless teenager; long, brownish-red hair reaching down the shoulders, left brown eye, right blue eye, and wore a black shirt with a blue waistcoat, beige pants, and black combat boots. In the background, it looked like she was in the Assembly Room of Independence Hall.

There was a date and time at the bottom left hand side of the screen that said, "February 22, 2013 at 10:22 a.m. EST." The recording took place 142 years back. Kent had a stunned expression on his face as if he recognized her from somewhere. Finally, the woman spoke, "Good morning. My name is Samuela Jereni Mentor. If you are watching this, then it's time for you to know the whole truth behind the Global Cataclysm and the Tribes of Libra. It may come as a shock to you, and you may not take this lightly."

Static interrupted before turning back to normal. We didn't know what happened with Riley's face-palming irritation. What the hell was going on? Was there some information missing, or was it just old? It didn't matter. We continued to watch the message as the person who called herself Samuela Mentor continued, "In the year 1993, my father Spiro created a secret science division that would enhance, manipulate, and evolve the human genome: Nova Vega. Before it became a country comprised of Thirteen Colonies of the United States of America, it was used as a science experiment facility to create a new breed of humans: Dúnami. Most of the test subjects— men, women, and children— died during the process when they were injected with Power Enhancement Serums."

Mrs. Valentine covered her mouth in devastation upon hearing the outcome of the injection process. Janice began puking, eyes watery and her face red and bloated. Samuela continued, as we listened, "Each of the colors would grant a test subject a supernatural ability beyond comprehension. So many failures, we were told, and according to the Aztec Prophecy mixed with the Mayan Calendar, that the world would face cataclysmic devastation, and time was running out. Fifteen years after many tests, I was the first subject to survive the injection process due to having a strong mind."

I noticed Kent's eyes widened with his jaws slightly dropped. Did he know this woman, or was it a coincidence? No time for answers at the moment, I looked back at the television screen to listen to Samuela. "The other subjects' minds weren't resilient enough to let it in due to strong resistance to the serum. Five more survived the process: Cedric Falco, Hironobu Mizuchi, Vivian Garcia, Bongani Chizoba, and Alice Harris. We trained for four years after I received a vision of the upcoming apocalypse, and we saved the world with the help of the other thirty-four subjects. We possessed more than one power and were dubbed Pasdúnami. But after Nova Vega went from a science division to a country, I discovered the terrible truth."

Much to our disappointment, there was more static. Irritated and impatient for having to wait through the interruption, Ferenc was about to pop the disc out until the screen turned back to normal. I rushed to my brother and grabbed his left arm, pointing out the solved problem; no more static.

Rolling his eyes in annoyance, Ferenc said that if there was more static, he would turn it off. Paying attention, we all continued to listen to Samuela. "The Nova Vegan government has no intention of stabilizing peace to its society and the world. It is carrying out the true agenda that's been forged by my father- Project Eden. It is a plan to purge the planet of what its creator believed to be imperfection and remake the world anew; but with Nova Vega as the new Garden of Eden and two surviving candidates to become the new Adam and Eve. Only at that time, would they be stripped of their free will, the very trait that was deemed the source of humanity's imperfection, during the global terraforming process. What he failed to realize is only Project Eden would destroy the world outside of Nova Vega, including those within Nova Vega and the government with it; catching them in an unexpected crossfire. They're blinded by their desire to become my father's Angels with him as the new God. By seeking to initiate the plan, he turned Libra into Perditus. My father wants to take the Maker's place.

"And I have also learned that my father was responsible for the Global Cataclysm, becoming a Pasdúnamis himself- dangerous, charismatic, and ultimately cruel and destructive. When we saved the world, we thought we had put an end to the apocalypse, but we were deceived. We only delayed the inevitable, and my father won't rest until he destroys the entire planet with the Second Global Cataclysm. If he is not stopped, there won't be a world to save anymore. Whoever is watching this message, you must go to the Hall of Freedom. The war with my father and the Nova Vegan government has begun. We must do whatever we can to fight back and give freedom back to Nova Vega and the world. May the Maker protect us all."

And with the message ended, the screen went black with only these words in the middle, "Message Ended." Kent and I glanced at one another. Our eyes widened and jaws dropped slightly before turning our attention back to the television screen.

XXIX- Kent Bernard

I couldn't believe it. That was the woman from my previous dreams. And the man that stood over her saying something about the Maker protecting her and her companions. That man was her father. But how was that possible? The message we saw was over a century old. Spiro Mentor would have to be dead by now, but she said that he's a Pasdúnamis himself. So maybe, it was possible that Spiro could've been one of the Immortals in that sense.

I looked at Mr. and Mrs. Valentine and asked, "Where's the central broadcast network?"

"In Manhattan, but it's heavily guarded and monitored by the Nova Vegan Secret Police," Mrs. Valentine answered.

Crossing his arms over his chest, Ferenc responded, "Except only one problem— parts of the message got scrambled, and we don't have all the information needed. There's gotta be more about what we don't know."

"It doesn't matter," said Phoebe. "As long as we know what we heard, that's all we need to know. That, and we'll have to get to the central broadcast network without getting caught."

"That would be a good idea," said a familiar voice. "But you can't."

We looked to the door, surprised to see it was my father. How did he find us? Did he track us? We didn't know, but I read his mind by glaring at him to see if he arrived to kill us, just in case. To my disbelief, he was here to warn us instead. By diving into his memories via telepathy, I learned that Hestia was responsible for freeing him from Rex's Sleeper Agent Serum, which was how the Angels of Death came into existence. And for the first time in my life, tears came from his eyes. He discovered what truly happened to Mom four years back. Reading his mind again, I learned why Rex would go so far to use Dad to kill her. He sought to destroy the rebel cell, thus stopping the mission of revealing the truth and Spiro's plans to all of Nova Vega. Not only that, but he was using Mom's inheritance to produce more Solaride, enough to make more weapons coated with that substance, and to kill the Pasdúnami.

"This is entirely my fault," said Dad. "I should've known that it was only a matter of time before Rex would go too far."

"Dad, none of it is on you," said Gabriella, as she walked to him.

"Gabriella is right," I said, showing my pity for him as I walked over. "Rex knew that with you around, he could not touch Mom. There was nothing we could've done."

Gabriella and I hugged our father to show that we forgave him for everything that had happened in the past four years, and he hugged back. I continued, "But if Mom and Aunt Tess were here right now, they would tell us to move on and finish what we started."

"But we can't," he said, as we stopped hugging. "They already know about the plan. In fact, they knew the moment Rex betrayed us, and the disc in *that* DVD Player is not safe here," he looked at Cali. "Neither is *her*," he looked at Seifer, "nor *him*."

Heads slightly tilting in confusion, Gabriella and I looked at Seifer with curiosity. The Aurora and the Valentine Siblings did the same thing. Could he be...? Seifer was nervous when we looked at him and asked, "What?"

"You didn't know?" Dad asked.

From what we learned from Dad that day, and through using my telepathy on Mr. and Mrs. Valentine, it turned out that Seifer was a Pasdúnamis, too. Even he was oblivious about it. They weren't being overbearing parents after all, much to my surprise. They were trying to protect him from the government and the secret police the whole time, much to Seifer's overwhelming disbelief.

When he was a year old, as Mr. Valentine told us, teleportation was his first power due to being part of the Teleporter Tribe. Mrs. Valentine mentioned that when their son was three years old, two more powers manifested in him; element manipulation and flight. Astonished, Seifer didn't remember at the time, until Dad read his parents' minds and learned of their overprotection. He was the only one in the family to be a Pasdúnamis. After thirteen years, they were expected to do the one thing that was difficult for them. They would have to let him go with the Aurora outside of the country. It was no longer safe for him, let alone for the disc, which he understood upon learning this revelation.

Janice didn't care what would happen to her. All she cared about was the government's destruction through the death of its chancellor. She cared about revenge more than she did her own safety and ours. But since things were going insane and volatile in Nova Vega, she was willing to make an exception, as long as she got the chance to fight another day. That was one argument even the Truman Siblings would not win. And for the record, she did find Phoebe and Ferenc's argument amusing.

Popping the disc out of the DVD Player, my sister placed it in my bag. The Valentine Family, with the exception of Seifer, teleported someplace safe,

135

possibly the Hall of Freedom. It was the one place where Mom, Dad, Adam, Mary, Joshua, Sarah, Tess, and Rex came from. The problem was that the Aurora and I weren't allowed to go there until another time. After learning that no place, including that place and the central broadcast network that weren't safe for us, I understood. Even Ferenc agreed, but only because the missing parts of the message irritated him. Dad told us, after walking to the window and pointing east, "There's a civilization outside of Nova Vega. It's located somewhere at the other side of the world."

He looked at us and placed his right arm down, much to mine and everyone's eye-widening astonishment. We never knew there were survivors outside of the walls before, until now. He continued, "It's populated by both Dúnami and Óchidunámei alike. All of them exiled and they are the survivors of the dying world. Find it and stay there until the time is right."

"What about you?" Janice asked.

"I will meet up with the surviving rebels at the Hall of Freedom to prepare for another war."

"Hold up," said Ferenc, as he grabbed my right shoulder hard.

I was not pleased with him when he did that, but he showed us a small, circular microchip that was blinking red as if it was detonating. He said that it was a tracking device, much to our surprise. Officer White must've placed it on me after I was sent back to my former cell in Nova Vegan Prison. So, it was official. His loyalty went to Chancellor Jelen. If she wasn't going to find the Aurora through my words, due to me not knowing where they went, she would have to place me under surveillance to find out their location. She was counting on me being rescued all along.

That was definitely not a good sign. Ferenc dropped it on the floor and crushed it underfoot. But it was already too late, as we turned to the sound of the sirens just outside the door. To our horror, and my heart-racing in disbelief, the secret police had already arrived. Startled by them breaking and entering the house, the secret police officers and the police officers alike were armed with batons and guns. Rex came in and Dad manipulated part of the wooden floorboard to materialize it into a sword-like baton.

He looked at me and ordered, "Kent, you, your sister, and all of your friends must leave the house," he looked at our enemies with fierce determination, "I will hold them off."

Desperate, I didn't want to leave him, but Ferenc grabbed hold of me as I watched my father battle Rex alone. And right before my eyes as we reached the sliding back door, the cruel captain, with a malevolent grin on his face, stabbed Dad through the heart. Blood splashed on my face and Ferenc's right arm, pounding in my ears as I watched with helplessness. With tears in my eyes, I let out a big NO, alerting the secret police as they started shooting at us. Gabriella and Riley looked stunned, too, but they manipulated the glass to materialize it into guns, aggressively shooting back before catching up with the rest of us. We barely escaped with our lives, avoiding incoming bullets.

***

Out of the sun room and through the pool area, we went to the Truman's RV at the driveway. Riley, who was reluctant at first to depart from his pet, said goodbye to Newt and teleported him to the same location where his other pets were. It was good that the RV had a bathroom, because my cousin needed to wash his hands.

Ferenc drove the RV out of the driveway and into the streets, heading straight for the airport, which was about an hour away and where we would use a plane to escape Nova Vega. It was a plan he came up with while I was away. We turned left out of the cul-de-sac, and we were on the highway, making a getaway from the secret police. While doing so, I sat on the chair at the table, feeling defeated.

Cali walked over and sat next to me, placing her hands on my shoulders. Emotionless, I didn't care. First, Mom. Now, Dad. My sister and I became orphans, and I was not happy about it. Riley being the only family we had left was not enough for me. I still couldn't believe my father was gone. Even after he was free from Rex's control, and I forgave him for everything wrong in my life, my time with him was short-lived.

"I'm sorry, Kent," she said. "There was nothing we could've done."

"Yeah," I responded.

"But your father made his choice, and he loves you and Gabriella very much. You said so yourself; your mother and aunt would want you to move on after they died. Now, he would want you to do the same."

"Yeah. You're right," I wiped my tears with my left hand before Cali removed her hands from my shoulders and got off the chair.

Getting off the chair, and pulling myself together for the groups' sake, the clothes I switched to, as I found them in the clothes cabinet next to the bathroom, was a green striped short-sleeve shirt with navy blue jeans, a black hooded cloak, and gray shoes. Janice got her turn and changed into a new set of clothes; a dark-red sleeveless shirt with a necklace containing a silver crucifix, black circular studs on her earlobes, black jeans, a black belt with a bronze belt buckle, and black combat boots reaching up toward her knees.

Before Seifer could have his turn with the change of clothes, there were gunshots coming from outside, startling us. He climbed up to the roof to find out what was going on. Seifer's eyes widened while looking back at us from the roof door.

"It's the secret police! We're being pursued!" he shouted.

We were all stunned, and Phoebe was the first to climb up to the roof to meet up with him. Janice was next because she was eager for a conflict. I was the last one to climb up. Those three would need my help in a highway battle.

***

There were a hundred secret police officers, including Rex and Officer White. They turned from the police force to a militaristic army. Surrounding us on both sides on the highway were tall trees, the sun barely visible with dark thunderclouds. And behind our enemies was a black limousine. My guess was that Chancellor Jelen was with them. I had never seen her in battle before, but Janice had, after trying to assassinate her once. Officer White took out his megaphone from the secret compartment located at the brake area of his hover motorcycle and said through it, "Stop the RV, Aurora! You have nowhere to go!"

In response, as Ferenc was still driving, Janice flipped the bird twice, one finger from each hand, and said to them, "Go to Hell!"

One of the officers shot at her, but only one bullet grazed her left cheek. It was a straight cut, but she chose not to have it healed. She's used to seeing them as battle scars. And it was a battle that we were about to engage in. My fist clenched, my eyebrows furrowed and I was prepared to make our enemies pay for what they'd done. Seifer manipulated the smoke from the roof pipe and materialize parts of it into a sword and gun. Janice and I did the same thing, but Phoebe took out her bow and Aduhim to morph it from a sword to twelve arrows.

Rex, after taking out his sword-like baton, looked at Officer White and said, "You deal with the Tele...no, the new Pasdúnamis and the Nova Vegan Rebel! I'll deal with Kent and Truman myself!" he said looking at the secret police. "The rest of you take down the RV!"

"No!" said Jelen coming from the roof window with a materialized sword at hand. "Janice Campbell is mine! It's time to settle the score with her and finish what I started five years ago!"

"Very well, Chancellor!"

Rex grabbed hold of Officer White, who took out his sword-like baton, and teleported to the RV roof. Jelen teleported to the roof as well, and four of us were ready to fight the three.

***

And while the secret police attacked the RV, Gabriella and Cali used the sink water to materialize bow and arrows and shoot at them through the window. Riley did the same thing, but materialized it into a gun. Ferenc manipulated part of the passenger's seat and materialized it into a handgun before shooting at the officers from the driver's window.

***

Seifer lost his grip on gun after he fell near the edge of the RV thanks to Ferenc focusing more on the officers and less on the road. Officer White held Seifer's

138

wrists down, but the latter kicked the cruel officer in the stomach. The malicious officer groaned and held his stomach before making a quick recovery while Seifer stood back up in determination to fight back. Some of the secret police officers climbed over the roof, and Phoebe shot them off, while I dealt with Rex myself. The officers that were shot either flew off their hover motorcycles, or incinerated on explosive impact. Those that flew off, splattered on hard concrete, slammed into other officers, or crashed into the limousine.

Rex had the upper hand when he attempted to slice my throat. Eyes widened in fright, I nearly felt the tip of the blade coming right at me before lifting myself back up. Outraged by what he almost did, and for the death of my parents, I manipulated the smoke and rammed some of it at his face in fury, causing him to scream in agony from the hot burns as he covered his face with his left hand. I put the gun away and took his sword-like baton. To my surprise, he had a second baton. Putting the sword away, my former uncle and I clashed batons. Phoebe shot more officers to protect me, Seifer, and Janice, using her telekinesis to retrieve her arrows in order to continue.

While Seifer teleported behind Officer White to punch him to unconsciousness, Janice and Jelen struggled with the swords; evenly matched from sword-clashing. The evil chancellor mocked Janice, taunting her, "How does it feel to be the only survivor? It must've hurt when your parents perished into oblivion."

Provoked with rage, the rebel's attacks were deadly beyond compare. Fast, ferocious, and fierce; each strike Janice made with her sword slashed through Jelen's skin from the hands; to her cheeks and to her right arm. Our ally was cut in the cheek right back, but grazed the cut she received from one of the bullets, forming an X-marked scar.

Just as Janice was about to strike her enemy down, one of the secret police officers shot the right front tire then the right back tire, causing it to spiral out of control. Then, as my allies and I reacted at the last minute, the RV flipped sideways, throwing off any officer attempting to climb on the RV to their death. Phoebe extended her wings to fly off the large, rolling vehicle. Thinking fast, I held on to Rex so we would fly off the roof together. Janice did the same to Jelen, while Seifer did his part with Officer White, who was the only one to have died on impact. The back of the officer's skull was cracked, while a majority of his organs ruptured; spewing blood from his mouth like vomit.

The rest of us survived, but were severely injured from landing on the pavement of the US-70 Bypass in Selma. I had a nosebleed, bruises, and my right leg had a large, bleeding cut at the calf. The limousine fell in the ditch leading to another highway below with the survivors of the battle fleeing for their lives. Phoebe landed on the ground to safety and hugged both me and Seifer, knowing that we were alright. Despite our injuries, we were relieved. Janice looked at

Jelen and picked up her sword. She stumbled on over to her enemy with one last attempt to end her life once and for all. The three of us noticed in worry, and Phoebe yelled, "Janice, don't! She's already beaten! Leave her be!"

"I can't!" Janice screamed in fury, before turning to us then back at Jelen, who was struggling to get back up. "*She* killed my parents, and she deserves to die for what she has done!"

"That may be true!" I said. "But if you kill her in hostility, you'll end up no better than her! Revenge won't bring your parents back, and there is no justice in that!"

Then, the RV, which was totally trashed, was hanging by the edge of the highway bridge. Gabriella, Riley, Cali, and Ferenc were still inside, and they were in serious danger! It could fall over any second and time was running out! Just when Seifer, Phoebe, and I went over there, Janice said to us, "What are you doing?!"

"Saving our friends' lives!" said Seifer, looking at her.

"You can't walk away now! We have to finish off..." she pointed at Rex and Jelen with her sword, "...*those* bastards once and for all!"

"Our friends' lives are more important!" I scolded. "If your family was in a situation like this, would you save them?!"

"But my parents are dead! I couldn't do anything to save them!"

"Then, this is the time to make up for lost time! You couldn't save them because you were young and weak! But that's all in the past! You can either help save our friends, or fulfill your revenge! The choice is yours and yours alone!"

The RV was already slipping, and startled by the sound of it screeching and scratching, Phoebe and Seifer manipulated the metal of the heavy vehicle with everything they had. Not a moment to lose, I jumped to the door. The inside of the mobile vehicle was in flames, and I coughed from the smoke. So, I managed to hold my breath to prevent the toxic fumes from going inside my body. The fire was too blinding for me to see four of my allies, but just when I was about to lose my breath, my eyes widened in realization from what I'd seen beyond the flames. Four of my allies survived the crash thanks to Gabriella projecting a water sphere, which also healed their injuries on the arms, legs, chest, and nose through each watery tentacle inside the burning RV.

I managed to teleport my sister over to Phoebe and Seifer with Riley as the second. Cali and Ferenc held their breath after the sphere evaporated, and she was the third person I saved. Ferenc was going to be the last person to save, but the RV was slipping further, indicating that Phoebe and Seifer had lost their grip. I was too afraid to teleport the both of us out there. We were about to die on impact on the I-95. But then, I felt a hand, and Ferenc and I were back on the bridge safe and sound. The RV was destroyed along with some of our stuff. Most of the food was gone, no clothes, and only several bottles of soda, juice, milk, and majorly water to help us survive. That sucks for the most part. Well, to our relief, at least the textbooks made it, along with the classified disc.

Turning around, it was Janice. She'd saved me and Ferenc from an explosive death. Judging by the smirk on her face, it was clear that she was reluctant to save the day at first, but after what I told her with Phoebe and Seifer at my side, Janice made her choice. But knowing her, she didn't do it because of us. She did it because she knew it was what her parents would want her to do. I wouldn't blame her. Her parents would be ashamed if Janice remained consumed with her obsession with revenge. But without the RV, there was no way to get to the airport.

"What are we going to do now?" Riley asked, as he looked at us in worry. "We lost our ride."

"Why not a limousine?" Janice asked, as she pointed at it.

Despite the minimal damage it received, it was also an excellent notion. It would be much faster than an RV anyway. Phoebe, Ferenc, and I used our telekinesis to levitate what was left of our stuff, and the rest of the group followed us to the slightly trashed limousine. A quick repair with our powers, and it would be good to go.

Then without warning, BANG! It was the sound of a gunshot, and it came from the angry Rex, who was bleeding from the top left side of his head and holding a gun. We looked at our chests, and we saw the one person he had shot—Seifer. Phoebe, in her grief, caught him before his head hit the pavement. He was shot directly in the descending aorta, near the bottom of his heart. Riley was going to heal the wound, but Rex laughed hard and shouted, "You can't heal people when they're minutes from death!"

"Then, I'll revive him!" Cali shouted.

"Don't you get it?! Even if you bring a person back to life, then what?! Look around you! *You're* the last Returner of Nova Vega! And if you die, who's going to revive you then?! The Maker?! Death happens all the time, and there is nothing you can do to stop it! Even if you could, there are always consequences for reviving the dead!" he pointed at Ferenc. "Look at what happened to *him* when he came back, after hearing him and his sister fighting and arguing, through the surveillance tracking device! He's more cynical than ever before! Resurrection always comes with side effects, whether all of you accept that part of reality or not! It always comes with a price! People would only live to die again!"

"Is that why Mom's body disappeared?!" I yelled. "Because you wanted to prove that deep down, resurrection brings nothing but misery and suffering?! True, it may give side effects to most people, but it also gives them a second chance in life! To help them live their life the fullest!"

Rex looked at me with hostility in his eyes and responded, "Just like Fedora, always overly optimistic, incapable of facing the true meaning of reality. No matter how much you hope, there will be no future for anyone! Not even for *you*! Even if the Maker knew they didn't deserve death, still," he aimed his gun at me, "it is better to face eternal unhappiness and shame! Give my regards to my sister and her husband!"

He was about to kill me, but I was pushed out of the way before he pulled the trigger. BANG! Looking up from the ground, and much to my mouth-gaping horror, the person that was shot was none other than Cali. She collapsed, and Riley hurriedly caught her in his arms. Rex, whom I looked at directly, gave a loud, cruel laugh, expressing a maniacal smile on his face as he boasted at the fact that he shot a Pasdúnamis with the ability to revive the dead. To him, it felt good, because he wanted to prove that no one should cheat death, even if their time had not yet come. To him, if the Maker couldn't take lives, then man would do it for Him. But to me, in my heartbreaking rage, he was taking away the very person who could help bring hope back to Nova Vega, as well as destroying the primary means of helping the world around us. Rex became a destroyer, another monster, another harbinger of death!

I stood from the ground and manipulated part of the concrete pavement to materialize a sword with a blade that glowed bright when the green button in the middle of the hilt was pressed once. It could also morph into a laser gun when I press the same button twice. I charged right at my enemy in full rage, blocking the bullets, almost hitting me when he shot at me, if not for my telekinesis. Tackling him hard, I teleported both of us into the middle of the parking lot in what was left of Rosewood High School, right before Jelen stood back up.

***

Rex managed to get his sword-like baton back after he and I flew off the roof of the RV, and both of us clashed our weapons. That time it was vicious and brutal. I was burning in rage for what he did to Mom, Dad, Aunt Tess, Seifer, Cali, and everyone he killed and sought to kill. He grabbed me by the throat and threw me into the destroyed library with his telekinesis. Books fell everywhere, computers were massacred, and tables were pushed backwards by a strong force like the wind in hurricane season; if we ever had one of course.

I managed to recover quickly and dashed toward him as he ran at me. We clashed like angry wolves fighting over their prey. He cut my back as we moved on to the demolished hallway, which was stained in dry blood with some of mine mixed with it. Running through the hallway, where a chemistry and art class were, we continued to clash swords. Pressing the button twice, my sword turned into a laser gun, and I managed to shoot through Rex's blade, damaging his right eye and partially blinding and bleeding him as a result. Screaming with a mixture of extreme pain and insane fury, he used his telekinesis to shatter window glass like a building exploding from the inside, then aimed them directly at me. I did the same, but I blocked the shattered glass with a bunch of lockers and two classroom doors.

The sword-like baton slashed through them, and I managed to dodge the blade by jumping further back. Entering what was left of the chemistry classroom, I noticed a bunch of chemicals, beakers, and test tubes. Using the table as a shield to keep Rex out of the classroom, I mixed chemicals that were never ever meant to be fused together; Nitric Acid and Hydrazine. I kept them apart long enough for my enemy to cut through. I pushed the chemicals toward him and mixed them as they got close to him, causing a mass explosion. The amount of force pushed me backwards out the window.

Unfortunately for me, Rex manipulated the fire from the explosion, surviving the impact. He used it to attack, but I managed to evaporate it with water from the grass, putting it out before bringing the plants back to life. He teleported in front of me to grab my throat so I wouldn't escape, then 2,000 feet above the parking lot, in which he managed to extend his pair of black bat wings beforehand, leaving me horrified at its demonic appearance. Before he had a chance to stab me in the chest, I quickly morphed the laser gun back into a sword and stabbed him in the arm, forcing him to release me from his grip as he screamed in further pain.

As I fell, I noticed Janice being injured in the right leg by Jelen, who was suddenly teleported here right after Rex and me. I was going to teleport to my ally, but my enemy grabbed me by surprise and threw me hard to the ground, causing me to lose my grip of my morph sword, partially damaging my internal organs. That was extremely painful. My body could barely feel anything, everything was spinning, and my nose was bleeding. I could barely stand on my feet. Instead, I fell on one knee, causing me to groan in pain. Rex descended from the sky, looking down on me like he was the victor. He aimed his sword-like baton at my neck, and Jelen, holding Janice by the hair, watched in pleasurable cruelty as I looked at the man that I once called my uncle.

"It is over, Kent," he said. "No one can protect you or anyone in Nova Vega now. You are weak, just like your parents," he said, raising his blade to force me to stand up without stabbing me. "I could've been the leader of the rebel cell. We could've ruled Nova Vega and all of Perditus. At least I agreed with Cyria before she was banished from the Hall of Freedom. Yes, she was the first to seek to conquer Nova Vega, and she did. And now, with Tess gone, I seek to rule it at the chancellor's side."

My eyes widened in disbelief when I heard the revelation of Chancellor Jelen. He smiled and lowered his sword.

"Oh, did your father and the other rebels neglect to tell you? Were you told too late?" he continued. "Cyria Jelen was to join in with Fedora and Jacob's rebel cell, until the Hall of Freedom discovered her treachery and banished her. So, I decided to carry out her legacy. And the worse part of all was that I was deeply in love with her. Not only did I show my loyalty to the chancellor by executing my own wife, but also showed her my true feelings for her. And you didn't know, and neither did your sister, nor your cousin. How delightful. Too bad for you, because you will lose everything."

"No...I...WON'T!!!" I said, as I jumped backwards away from Rex. "You both want to be together?! I'll be happy to oblige!"

I used all of my might to manipulate the soil, bricks, concrete, grass, and fences. Before I knew it, I developed the ability to animate. I animated people in the form of my parents, only the upper bodies from head to belly made of soil with hair of grass and concrete eyes, and 2,000' in height. The giant animated replica of Mom had fence-like eyelashes and lips made of bricks. The weird part was that instead of using just one power, I used two powers all at once. I levitated Rex and Jelen, who were stunned and dismayed by what I could do before Janice was released from the latter's grip. Through my powers, I made the giant animated replicas of Mom and Dad close their hands on two of my frightened enemies, sealing them inside like a caterpillar crystalizing within its cocoon. The fingers were left open to let them breathe. Rex and Jelen's lives were not mine to take. But it was my parents' retribution to them. That was more than enough for me.

As I collapsed, Janice, who healed her leg, caught me. Using two powers at once took a lot out of me. Either that, or I lost some of the blood from my back. Either way, I was relieved to know that I (or we) won the battle. Janice healed my back along with the rest of my body, and we teleported to the limousine, where the Aurora awaited our return from our final confrontation.

XXX- Kent Bernard

The ticket agent that Ferenc ordered tickets from was a Pasdúnamis, and she was Adam and Mary's ally according to their son. She had the abilities of telepathy, foresight, flight, and teleportation. And regardless of Seifer and Cali dying from their wounds, which were covered from front to back, I applied pressure to prevent more bleeding. She was just as worried as the rest of us, gave us a separate jet; an emergency for the Truman Siblings, she said, in case they were in any danger from our enemies.

That was a nice occasion from Raleigh-Durham International Airport. Too bad the government wouldn't be missing their limousine. For all we knew, they had more. Dang, Chancellor Jelen! Cheapskate much?! That, and because Seifer and Cali were slowly dying, it was better for them to pass on outside of Nova Vega than inside it. Die free people than die slaves. Sad, but worth it.

***

Inside the plane was a massive room with eight spinning chairs; four on each side, a bed at the very back, a lavatory, a kitchen by the same lavatory, baggage bay under the bar next to the lavatory door, and a cockpit in front. After we went inside the plane and took flight, Ferenc changed out of his school uniform into his gray shirt with black short sleeves, blue jeans, and black shoes. We looked out the window to make certain that we weren't spotted. Our best advantage was the clouds, and we saw the ocean on the other side of the wall. But, to our wonder, it was brownish-red like blood. No matter what lied beyond the wall, we had to keep going. There was no turning back for any of us now. It was now, or never.

Reaching outside of Nova Vega, we heard the alarm system, triggered by our departure. The government and the secret police went on high alert as we were close to the clouds. The surface-to-surface missiles were being launched, and as we feared for the worst, Ferenc told us to fasten our seatbelts. Four of the missiles were on our tails, and he spun the jet in an attempt to get them to destroy each other. It succeeded for three of them, but one more was left. We were out of options. Eyes widened, Phoebe and I looked at one another, and I asked, "Are you thinking what I'm thinking?"

"I am," she answered. "It's going to be insane, but it should work."

Smirking, I said, "I was thinking the same thing."

The Aurora looked at the two of us in disbelief after we unbuckled ourselves. Ferenc noticed us unbuckling and told us to "sit back down" as we rushed to the emergency exit.

We didn't listen to him, instead jumping out. Phoebe extended her wings and carried me from under my arms. I manipulated the missile to slow it down and aimed directly at the launchers, which contained dozens of Nova Vegan Security Guards. They were already on the enemy's side anyway. I reversed the firing course with my telekinesis and aimed the palm of my hands directly at the base, causing the final missile to fly directly at the launcher, blowing it up to kingdom come, killing several of the guards and injuring the rest before they had time to escape. The Aurora was safe, and Phoebe and I went back inside the plane before it went inside the clouds.

***

And for once, Ferenc's irritation was only brief. Turns out that Rex was not entirely correct. Even if Phoebe's brother came back from the dead, it didn't mean he was a complete jerk. Either that, or his mentality just needed time to recover. No one knew what the outcome would be upon resurrection, as long as that person was given a second chance at life. Ferenc was very proud of what Phoebe and I had accomplished. It was strategic and wise. Insane, but strategic and wise.

But that moment of cheer was cut short as everyone's sadness, including mine, returned. Seifer and Cali, side-by-side in bed, were still dying from the gunshot wounds they received from Rex back at the highway. We had no choice but to say our tearful farewell to them, and we started with Seifer. Phoebe held Seifer's hand, shedding tears as she watched his heavy breathing. He gave a little smile and said, "Don't feel bad."

"But I didn't want you to die," Phoebe responded back with a broken voice.

"I know. From the moment I met you, I was in love with you. But now, you must move on to someone else," he looked at me as I walked over to him and got on my right knee. "Kent, take good care of her."

Nodding with my share of tears, I responded sadly, "I will."

"Thank you," he looked back at Phoebe. "Farewell, Pheebs. See you around."

And just like that, he closed his eyes and produced his last breath. He was gone. Phoebe cried, burying her head in the empty shell's chest. Ferenc, who set the plane to auto-pilot, placed his hands on her shoulders, trying to comfort her. I went to Cali, who was going to die, with a minute or two left to live. But I felt nothing but guilt for what she did for me, sad that I may never see her kind, warm smile again. She was my first love, but it was over. Rex was right. She was the last Returner of Nova Vega. She was also the only Returner in the Aurora.

Without her, we were on our own. We would have to make sure we survive, endure, and live.

I kneeled next to her and held her hand. She looked at me with that same smile on her face. And it was the last smile that I was going to see before she passed on. Finally, with a sad frown on my face and heartbreaking despair pouring in my mind, I said, "I should've been the one to take the bullet."

"Had you done so, Rex would've killed us all," said Cali. "You, Phoebe, and the Aurora must live. You six must look after one another. I took the bullet to help you guys survive and fight another day. Now, before I go, I have something to give you as a token of my good will."

She took out that something from her pants pocket and placed it in my hand. It was a brass key in the shape of a cross. I had never seen it before. She continued, "My parents gave this to me before they were arrested and killed. They said that it is very important. I don't know what it does, but I hope you'll find some use for it," she looked at Phoebe. "*She* loves you very much, you know," she said looking at me, coughing. "Don't worry about me. Worry about yourself and the Aurora."

"Will I ever see you again?" I asked, tears streaming from my eyes.

"I have a feeling we will."

"Then, we'll meet again in the Afterlife."

"And I'll be waiting. Farewell, Kent Tavi Bernard, and thank you...for everything."

With her last breath and eyes closed, she was gone. Two members of the Aurora departed from the Material World and into the Invisible World. Hopefully, she was reunited with her parents. Like Phoebe, I, too, mourned, covering my face with both hands as I cried. Gabriella and Riley were there for me, comforting me, trying to help me cope with what had passed as they hugged me from behind.

***

We made it to the other side of the world that evening. But the private jet ran out of gas and descended. Ferenc made a safe landing in the calming, sunny sand at the last minute, saving us from what would've been a plane crash. There was no sign of civilization and no time to search for the one Dad told us about yet. Near the shores of the Persian Gulf, we gave Seifer and Cali a water funeral. The water was clear enough, unlike the Atlantic Ocean, and we materialized the sand and water we manipulated into coffins. The bottoms of the coffins were smooth wood with the cover made of indestructible crystal glass and shaped like a dome. Those coffins were special, for they preserved the corpses to last forever. The bodies of Seifer and Cali laid straight with their hands over their hearts in the form of peaceful slumber. Tears rolled from my eyes in sadness when they left us, but I was also happy to know that their suffering was over.

They departed further, further, and further, until they vanished from sight into the horizon. Getting out of the water, I walked to the top of the mount of sand among the Aurora, saying to them, "We're finally free from Nova Vega. Even when Seifer and Cali died, they died free people. It is what all of us wanted: Freedom. Now, we must search for the Exiled Colony. We don't know where it's at, but if it takes the rest of our lives to find it, so be it. If we don't find it, Seifer, Cali, Dad, Mom, Aunt Tess, and many others would've died for nothing. We won the battle, but the war has only begun. For now, we must lay low until the commotion in Nova Vega dies down. We don't know when that'll happen and how. If we have to remain away from the place of our birth for the rest of our lives, then we will do so. Until the time comes, we move forward."

Phoebe, despite knowing that she might not see her parents again, was willing to go along with me. Gabriella may have been alone without me for the past three years, but she had no intention of being alone again. Riley supported my decision to look for the Exiled Colony since he didn't want to live in a country monitored by the man that he once called his father. Ferenc was still cynical about what I did, even before he came back from the dead, nevertheless, he chose to go wherever his sister goes. Janice was still focused on wanting Chancellor Jelen dead, but she was more than eager to come along.

The Aurora was now a group of fugitives of Nova Vegan Law and traitors of Nova Vega. We were the exiled now. There was no turning back for us. We would hide among the Exiled Colony, and our search would begin with going to the northwest. The desert would not stop us from reaching our destination. Tomorrow, we would have to confront the Nova Vegan government again. But for today, our pursuit for the Exiled Colony begins.

End of Book I

Acknowledgements

Dear readers,

First of all, I would like to say thank you for your support in this story. Without you, none of this would ever have been possible. It wasn't easy, but I managed to pull through in the past four years of the story's development.

I couldn't have done this without my parents, first of all. My mother, God rest her soul, for installing story writing habits into my life. Despite our differences and viewpoints about life, reality, and the world around us, my father supported me the most when all seemed lost, including his part in the logo and cover art fundraiser at Ko-Fi and hiring three editors and proofreaders- Maria Catlett, Judi Blaze, and Cynthia Anaya.

Speaking of Ko-Fi, there are many other supporters there that helped me out to raise enough for both the *Thaumaturgic* cover art and the Creasurgence Entertainment company logo. These contributors are: Ben Fuller, Midokami (who made the suggestion of doing the fundraiser at Ko-Fi in the first place), Stu Tiger, Kevin Hendricks, Cameron Hops, Oni F. Mutt-Clarke, two Tigers (Bluish-Grey and Orange), Wyvrn Ripsnarl, Sammy Frostpaw-Bigbear, Meta Fur, Magico, Kumori Urufu, Jeremy Todd, Tkia Brown, and my relatives (paternal-Uncle Mike; maternal- Grandma Julie, Uncle Dan, Aunt Mary, and Cousins Erin & Brendan). The guy behind the cover art itself was Robet Xu, otherwise known as whiteguardian of DeviantArt (You guys should check it out. He made amazing artwork, including book covers.). Katty Wampus did an excellent job on the company logo, for without her, neither the trademark, nor the website would ever come to be. Also, one of my friends, Ryan Gates, also known as Tyrnn Eaveranth, helped me with the website publication issues when I was having trouble publishing creasurgence.com.

My main inspirations for this debut novel are Suzanne Collins's *The Hunger Games*, Lois Lowry's *The Giver* & *Gathering Blue*, and George Lucas's *Star Wars*. While Lucas was actually the first writer (well, filmmaker, technically) to introduce me to the dystopian genre, I wasn't aware of what it was, or the term of it, as the time, until Collins. Lowry was the one who helped broaden my mind on the subject further. My muse for the character Janice Campbell was *Divergent* author Veronica Roth, who was also the main reason I started writing the first part of *The Thaumaturgic Trilogy*. As for the concept of superpowered humans in the story, I have Marvel's *X-Men* and Sucker Punch's *inFamous* to thank for that.

The names of the characters' pets, on the other hand, the idea of naming them after fictional characters came from my late cat Cookie, who was named after Crookshanks from *Harry Potter*. The difference is, unlike in real life, the animals in Thaumaturgic was named after deceased characters from dystopian genre works. Kinda makes ya wonder why the Aurora and their allies would name their pets after the late characters in other works that are already out.

Speaking of dystopia, I would also like to thank Nicole Sidhu, my Women in Literature professor at East Carolina University, who also taught us about it through Margaret Atwood's *The Handmaid's Tale*, and the consequences of what would happen if we don't change our ways. And she's right. If the wrong course of action isn't averted, same thing could happen in real life (Thanks for the warning, Dr. Sidhu!).

Anyway, thank you all again for helping making this book into a reality. And I hope you can continue to support me as the series progress. Thank you, everyone.

May the Creator of All Existence guide you,

Merlin Patrick O'Toole